WONDER

A Richard Jackson Book

WONDER

Rachel Vail

Orchard Books   New York

Orchard Books
387 Park Avenue South, New York, NY 10016

Manufactured in the United States of America
Book design by Mina Greenstein
The text of this book is set in 12 point Fairfield Medium.
10 9 8 7 6 5 4 3 2 1

Library of Congress Cataloging-in-Publication Data
Vail, Rachel. Wonder : a novel / by Rachel Vail.   p.   cm.
"A Richard Jackson book"—P. preceding t.p.
Summary: Everything changes for twelve-year-old Jessica when
she enters junior high school and finds herself a social outcast,
ignored by all her former friends.
ISBN 0-531-05964-2.   ISBN 0-531-08564-3 (lib. bdg.)
[1. Friendship—Fiction.   2. Schools—Fiction.]   I. Title.
PZ7.V1916Wo   1991   [Fic]—dc20   91-10576

To MOM, DAD, and JON—
my favorite people on the planet

JUNIOR HIGH SUCKS. I can't believe it. I was so psyched to get here, and now I wish I'd never left sixth grade. The worst part of it all is, I don't really see how it's going to get any better. Or how I'm going to take much more. My life has been ruined by a thing called SCANTA.

What really gets me is Sheila. She was supposed to be my best friend. I mean, we've been best friends forever, or at least since kindergarten. But this summer she went to Camp Nashaquitsa with all of *them*. Camp changes people. I'm never going to sleep-away camp, even if my parents let me. I don't care. I've seen what camp does to a person.

Last year I was popular. Maybe not the most popular girl at Rand Elementary School, but reasonably popular. I didn't have to worry that nobody'd show up for my birthday party, and I always knew I'd have somebody to sit with at lunch even when Sheila was absent, which was pretty often. Her parents keep her home if there's a good old movie on TV. Seriously. But anyway, I was in the popular group. Had inside jokes, got chosen in the top five or six in gym even in sports I wasn't that good at. . . . Oh, God! Tomorrow we have gym. I'll be picked last. I'll be picked after Wheezy! No, it's not that bad. Please tell me it's not that bad. Maybe we could move. Maybe my parents will come upstairs right now and tell me to start packing, we're moving to California. Or Alaska. I don't care—Iowa. Just somewhere they haven't heard of SCANTA.

That's their name. Is that the stupidest? SCANTA. Sheila–Cathy–Andi–Nancy–Tracy–Amy. SCANTA. Makes me want to puke. They all wore red sweatpants and white Izods to school today. Oh, and black high tops. Nobody told me, of course. I wore the most ridiculous thing ever designed, produced, bought, or worn.

My mom and I went shopping last week. I wanted to go to the junior department, which is logical for going to junior high. The saleslady said, "Aren't you darling? But why don't you try preteen, dear?"

I was so humiliated. I mean, this pink-haired, mustache-lipped, bug-eyed woman was staring down over her mountain range of a bust line, literally checking out my bod. I swear! I felt naked. She scrutinized the place where my bust would be if I had anything—for five minutes, it felt like. Honestly, Dolly Parton would look like a first-grade boy next to that lady.

I'm no Dolly Parton, believe me. I don't even wear a bra yet, though I'm thinking about it. So what if I'm a little small for my age? I am almost thirteen years old, not nine or six! I have every right to shop in juniors. It's the *teen* department and I'm almost thir*teen*.

So my mom and I were walking away from her when I said, "Officious broad," and I thought my mother was going to pee herself. That's how hard she was laughing. I'm not exactly clear on what it means, but I've heard my father say it about people like that lady. Everybody was staring. Mom couldn't stop laughing. She held her hand over her mouth and pinched her nose shut, because her nostrils flare out when she laughs and her older sister teased her about it when she was a kid. Now she's a big-shot New York shrink, but she still pinches her nose when she laughs.

When she finally regained control, Mom said, "Well, she can't tell us where to shop. I'm sure we can find something smashing for you right here." She talks a little too dramatically sometimes, but still, she's pretty cool. She could've just walked right across the hall to preteen, but she understands about these things.

We looked for about an hour. There isn't a very large selection of size ones in Bloomie's Junior Department. I tried them all on. We finally settled on this sweatshirt-dress—white with different colored polka dots. I've got decent legs, so that's what we decided to "emphasize." To be honest, I thought I looked pretty good. Almost sophisticated. We got new socks to match, and new Keds, and this morning, when I left for school, I felt sharp. Until I saw SCANTA, that is.

I guess the first hint was Sheila. I called her yesterday to see if she wanted to walk together. She lives just up the street, and the junior high is five blocks away. We walked there one time last spring, talking about how it would be the first day we did it for real, which should have been today. But when I called, Sheila said she already had a ride from Tracy's mom. I felt sort of bad, but I didn't really think about it much because I was busy organizing my drawers.

I said I'd meet her by the entrance and we could walk into school together just like we did the first day of every year I can remember. I was hanging out there alone this morning, trying to look like I didn't mind. Two minutes before the bell, SCANTA showed up. One tight clump of red sweatpants and white Izods and black high tops. Everybody was looking at them, and they knew it. They loved it. They were walking into junior high like they owned it—like they were ninth graders instead of seventh. SCANTA. Yesterday I never heard of it. Today they took over the world.

I just stood there. It suddenly occurred to me that there was no way Sheila was going to break away and run over to me. I started to shake, waiting for I don't know what. SCANTA stopped in front of me—that's something, I guess. They didn't even look at anybody else. I managed a weak, general hi.

Nobody said hi back. Sheila pretended to be studying the concrete, stabbing it with her new high top. Finally Tracy looked at me with her icicle blue eyes and said, "Nice dress." Amy, Andi, and Nancy giggled a little. Cathy just held her clarinet case and looked blank, as usual.

"Thanks," I said.

Tracy said, "Looks like a Wonder Bread explosion!"

Wonder Bread. I knew when Mom pulled the dress off the rack it reminded me of something, and now I knew what—the wrapper of Wonder Bread, the shiny white plastic wrapper with the bright blue, yellow, and red polka dots. And there I was, trapped like a loaf of white bread inside it.

As I watched all their faces burst into laughter, for some reason I started thinking about the time I went to Jones Beach with my cousin Audrey. She took me in the waves for my first time, over the objections of my mother. I heard Mom standing on the beach, yelling, "Don't let go!" Was she talking to me or my cousin? I didn't ever think of that until today, with SCANTA laughing in my face. But somehow, we lost our grip on each other, my cousin and I, and suddenly I was tumbling, crashing into the sand, spinning. Didn't know which way was up. The noise was so weird—like being inside a vacuum cleaner, but also so quiet I could hear my pulse. I remember panicking, thinking I might never breathe again.

It was the same feeling today outside school. Even the noise. Looking back, it's hard to believe I stayed standing. I was spinning, tumbling, crashing, but I just stood there. The difference was, this time there were no hands pulling me out, toweling me off, pouring me a sandy Hawaiian Punch. Just Tracy. Screeching like she'd just said the funniest thing in the history of the world. And SCANTA, repeating, "Like a Wonder Bread explosion!" as they ran down the hall, laughing their collective head off.

 **2**

WHEN I GOT HOME from school, my brother, Benjamin, was already sitting at the kitchen table, dunking cookies and telling every detail of his day to Mom and Dad. Mom always comes home early the first day of school so she won't miss out. She's jealous that Dad gets to be home for us every day after school, since he has a deal with his partner, Uncle Tommy, to work 6:00 A.M. to 2:00 P.M. He makes panty hose for fat women. They're called Big N Pretty, and I can't think of a more embarrassing occupation. He wanted to be an astronaut.

Dad said, "So how's my favorite junior high student on the planet?" but I was already heading right up the stairs to get out of that dress. What a switch.

Usually I'm the one spilling my guts, and Benjamin is upstairs alone.

Mom yelled up, "Come on, Jessica! Topsy-Turvy Day!"

"Not me!" I yelled back, getting in my bed.

"Jessica, we been waiting for you!" Benjamin said.

"Benjamin," I answered, in Mom's I'm-trying-to-be-patient voice, "I am not in the mood. You guys can go without me."

"Well, that's no fun," said Dad.

"Tough darts," I said. That's Mom's expression. Nobody knows where she got it. I think "darts" is a way of avoiding saying "shit," but that's what it means.

I heard Dad coming up the steps to my room. "What's wrong, sweetheart?" he asked.

"Nothing. I just don't want ice cream before dinner. Is that a problem?" I didn't want to be fresh. I wanted to tell them everything that had happened and have them make it all better, but I was too humiliated. I just wanted to be alone.

"Why don't you come for the ride, then? Come on, it's a Powers family tradition. We want to have some special family time."

"Well, I don't," I said, and pulled my comforter over my head.

"Life is tough," he said. "Now get your shoes on and come downstairs."

Life is tough? Nobody has ever said anything so

8

cruel and heartless to me—not even Tracy. If he only knew what happened to me today, he'd feel so guilty, saying that. I put my new Keds back on and then wrote "Life is tough" on an index card with "Remember September 9" on it and put it in my newly cleaned-out top desk drawer. This way I'll remember, and someday when his entire world is collapsing on him, I'll say, "Dad, life is tough." See how he feels.

Before I went downstairs, I looked at myself in my new full-length mirror. I had forgotten I was still wearing that awful dress, the root of all my problems. I ripped it off, stuffed it in my backpack, and pulled on shorts and Dad's ugly old Big N Pretty sweatshirt. I'll dump the disgusting dress in the Rosensweigs' garbage can down the street tomorrow morning on the way to school. The Rosensweigs don't have any kids, so I don't feel guilty, like someone will think a kid of theirs was foolish enough to wear such a thing. I may be a social outcast, but at least I'm not completely inconsiderate.

I know Mom'll ask me about the dress soon during one of our private talks, and she'll probably be really mad because it cost a lot, but at this point I don't care. She didn't tell Dad how much it cost. "Just our secret," she whispered, and at the time I felt so grown-up and so loved. Now I feel like I hate her, even though deep down I know all this isn't really her fault.

3

MOM STILL HASN'T asked me about the dress. We haven't had a private talk all week. All her energy is being used up on Benjamin because he cursed at Ms. Fox and got suspended yesterday. Every fourth grader at Rand wants to curse at Ms. Fox (she's just that kind of person), but the difference is, Benjamin actually does it. It must be embarrassing for my mom to get called in to see the school shrink so often about her own son. He's a really weird kid—mostly he just sits without moving or making a sound and, with his white blond hair and huge brown eyes, he looks like a Kodak Christmas ad. But then sometimes, for no reason at all, he's screaming and cursing and flailing all over the place. Mom says he'll grow out of it. She's been saying that since he was two and a half.

I know, I know. Benjamin's problems are a lot bigger than mine. So what if I'm a social leper? At least I don't get suspended the second week of school. I've never even been sent to the principal. Other than being a reject, my life has never been anything but completely ordinary. I could just puke. I'm a good girl—not excellent, and certainly not popular, but a good girl. I feel bad for Benjamin, but I'm also jealous. He's James Dean. I'm Betty Boop. Well, at least I dress the part.

I've been trying to look more normal, but it's not easy to keep up without looking like I'm copying, and Mom won't let me wear sweatpants to school. I think maybe she would if I told her what's going on, but I just can't. I want her to think at least one of her kids is regular and happy and well-adjusted.

SCANTA got pink baseball hats. They put their ponytails through the back window of them, all except Andi, who has short hair. But she has the same walk and talk and giggle as the rest of SCANTA, so I guess hair length doesn't matter. Andi and I were friends in day camp together when she first moved here after her parents got divorced, and in fact I was the one who introduced her to everybody at the start of fourth grade. She was nervous that people wouldn't like her because she's black. She said she was lucky to have me as a friend. Now she's in SCANTA, so she doesn't talk to me anymore, either.

When I was walking home today, I wished for Mom and Dad to get divorced like Andi's and Tracy's and Cathy's and everybody normal's parents, but I didn't really mean it. They're having a fight about how to handle Benjamin. It's the only thing they ever fight about. I hate when they yell at each other—what if they really do get divorced, and I wished it on them, just so I could fit in? Usually they flirt. It's embarrassing. People used to tease me about it in school—"Jessica's parents make out with each other. . . ." What could I say? It's true! When she gets home, he meets her in the front hall and, honest to God, they make out. My *parents*. Gross.

But tonight they're fighting about Benjamin again. They think we can't hear them with their door closed, but we can. Benjamin doesn't care. I think he likes the attention. It's 11:11, my favorite time, and my light is still on, but nobody has come to tell me to put down my book and go to sleep. I've become invisible.

4

I SAT ALONE at lunch again today. Everybody's worst nightmare. I pretended I was so into reading my book that I didn't want to be bothered even unwrapping my tuna sandwich, not that I read word one. I just watched all the little letters dance around until I got too dizzy and closed my eyes and wondered if I'm losing my marbles. The insides of my cheeks are all messed up from where I was chomping down, but no way was I giving anyone the satisfaction of seeing me cry. Sheila looked over at me once and smiled. I wanted to punch her. I wanted to smile back to show I didn't even notice anything different was going on, to prove that it wasn't me calling her house and hanging up after she said hello when I couldn't think of how to ask why she stopped being my best friend. I wanted to show her that I knew about their stupid party and wouldn't go even if I *was* invited. But I couldn't smile. I just turned away.

Mom asked me tonight how come I don't invite Sheila over. She misses her, she said. I just shrugged. What was I supposed to say? "Mom, your only daughter has developed into a social outcast. There will be no more friends over. There will be no parties. She will never get married because nobody will ever like her and she will live miserably with you until she is a lonely old spinster and dies." Sure. Maybe I'm dying. Maybe I have some awful disease and they'll discover it soon and I'll be so brave, lying there in the hospital, that they'll put me on Oprah and make a TV movie about me and then Sheila will realize the error of her ways and come crying back to me, begging for forgiveness. And maybe I'll forgive her. Maybe. Does she ever think about me? I wonder.

Ugh! That word! I can't even think it without feeling like I'm going to throw up. That's what they call me now all the time. Wonder. And I thought *Jessica* was the worst—going through life with a name that has *sick* in the middle. I get to school, and there's SCANTA, hanging out by their lockers (they all got lockers next to each other, of course), giggling about inside jokes. Until I pass by. Then they shut up. Not that they're scared of me or anything—ha! Don't I wish that were it. No, they shut up out of respect for

14

my Daily Dose of Humiliation (DDH). Tracy looks right at me with her icicle eyes and very sweetly says, "Hello, Wonder." Sheila just looks down at her cool black high tops and blushes, but the rest of them all laugh. Maybe there will be a nuclear war tonight, and I won't have to go to school tomorrow.

It's just that, well, I never thought this could happen to me. People like Wheezy spend their whole life outside it all, so they get used to it. I'm new at this, and it's killing me. If this is puberty I could do without it.

Sheila probably thinks I haven't even heard about her party. That's why she smiled at me. Pity? Please, God, no. Or superiority? She wouldn't just sit there gloating, would she? I started to think, No, that's not like her, but then I remembered I really don't know her anymore. It's not for a birthday or anything. Sheila's just having a party a week from tomorrow, and boys are going. They're supposedly trying to keep it quiet because only certain people are invited. I'm not. They're so subtle, too. Talking about it until people who aren't invited walk by. Like we don't know. Right. We rejects hear everything—who's bringing what music, what they're wearing, what games they'll play. . . .

Kissing games, that is.

Last year Conor O'Malley had a graduation party, coed. He had decorated his basement by putting up tinfoil, streamers, and pink light bulbs. It was sort of funny, but I liked it anyway. The strangest part was, the girls were all bunched up on one side of the basement and the boys were on the other. I mean, we'd all been going to Rand together forever, and since we got over the cooties stage in fourth grade nobody has made that big a deal over sitting with the boys. But suddenly, at Conor's party, there was this weird tension. His mom brought down the cake and then went upstairs, leaving us unsupervised. The boys were getting rowdy on their side of the room, shoving their shoulders into one another and laughing. I remember having to go to the bathroom really bad, but there wasn't one in the basement and the stairs were on the boys' side. There was no way I was crossing through there, so I resolved to hold it. I didn't know why I felt so nervous, but I knew everybody else was tense, too. Finally Conor picked up an empty bottle of 7-Up from the "bar" he had set up, and put it on the floor. He came over to us and said, "Who wants to play Spin the Bottle?"

We got hysterical. Right in his face. I guess it wasn't such a funny thing to say, but at the time none of us could stop giggling. Conor turned hot pink but just kept standing there. I wonder (ugh) why. Maybe he was embarrassed to return to his side of the room, to retreat in defeat. Maybe he was so cool he was just waiting until we immature little girls got hold of ourselves. Or maybe he just froze, like I did the first day of school this year.

Finally, Sheila said, "Sure, let's play." That shut us up quick. She marched over and sat down, cross-legged, on the floor near the bottle, all by herself. Everybody, boys included, stared at her. Did they think she was a sex maniac, desperate to be kissed, or just a cool girl, willing to play whatever the host suggested? Then she called me over, and all eyes went to me. She didn't ask pleadingly or anything. She just said, "C'mon, Jessica," completely confident that I wouldn't leave her hanging. I could've, now that I think about it, and boy, would she have been humiliated. But I'm a better friend than that. So I went right over, cheeks burning Embarrassment Red (new Crayola color, when I become president of the company), and sat down next to her. Everybody else filled in around us.

Conor liked Sheila, and everybody knew it. I liked Conor, and nobody knew it. Not even Sheila. I have never admitted it out loud, or even in my journal, except in code. Not that he's ugly or anything. Okay, he looks a little like Howdy Doody, but he plays soccer, so he has a good body, and besides—I don't know—there's just something about him. The boy everybody admitted to liking is Conor's best friend, Jordy Roberts. Jordy is very good-looking. He's so quiet it's hard to hear him even on the rare occasions when he actually talks, but he's got green eyes, and shiny brown hair that hangs over them just a little, and this electric smile that makes even teachers blush. I knew all the girls wanted the bottle to point at Jordy for them, but I was secretly wishing for Conor.

Conor spun first, and the thing landed right between me and Sheila. I thought I was going to hyperventilate. Everybody was yelling and laughing and arguing over who it was pointed at. Sheila just sat there with her eyebrows raised. She looks really pretty when she does that. I knew I was turning Eleanor Roosevelt (Embarrassment Red) again. I blurted out, "I think it's pointed at Sheila!" What a jerk. It really was a speck closer to me, and I knew it. But I didn't want to seem overanxious. I had kept my crush a secret for so long I wasn't about to blow it then. What was I supposed to do, wrestle my best friend for the chance to kiss my Orange Crush?

That's what I call Conor in my journal. I have code names for everybody and lots of things—like if I want to write that I was really embarrassed I say I was Eleanor Roosevelt for Embarrassment Red. This way if I die and they discover my journal, nobody will know what or who I was writing about. I don't need my private life publicized all over the place.

Orange Crush is the perfect code name for Conor O'Malley because he is my crush and he is orange. His hair, I mean. Some people don't like that, but I honestly think it's cute. He has freckles, but not covering his entire face like his little brother Sean—just a small patch over the bridge of his nose. And blue eyes and a smile, not electric like Jordy's, but one that looks like he just got away with something devious. Plus, he is incredibly smart, without being geeky. Especially in math—but actually he's smart in everything. We're in all the same classes this year (except gym and Spanish) because I'm pretty smart, too, but Conor is the smartest in the whole grade. He doesn't show off or anything—he can't help being smart any more than Nancy can help being stupid. Or pretty. He's just smart, and it doesn't make him a geek at all. At least not to me.

But I made him kiss Sheila. I hated myself for it, but I did it anyway. When he looked at me after I said it was pointing at Sheila, I couldn't tell what he was feeling. Regret? Relief? He crawled across the circle and kissed her, really lightly, on the lips. I watched. Well, I couldn't help it, could I? I mean, I was sitting right next to her. I watched and tried to imagine what it would feel like to be Sheila right then.

Then it was Sheila's turn to spin, and she got Miles Crenshaw, who is nice but more as a friend. He lives next door to her and they played together growing up so it could have been like kissing your brother, but he's pretty easygoing and he made it not too awkward. We played for about an hour. By then it was starting to get boring and anyway it was time to go. My dad was the first there to pick up, as usual. I got kissed twice, both times by Miles, and it was no big deal. It was like being bumped into.

That was my first and only boy-girl party, and my first and only kissing experience. Next Friday is the first party of my junior high career, and I'm thinking of entering a convent because if I'm never invited to parties I'm never going to get kissed and I might as well start coping with the fact.

5

SHEILA'S PARTY is five days away now, and it has become clear to me that the only invitations I will ever get are to family parties. Like it or not, relatives are stuck with me.

Dad didn't want to go to the party at Gram's yesterday, either. I could tell. He's been working late every day this past week. It makes him a total grouch. I think something is going wrong for him at Big N Pretty. He used to be home after school to joke around with me and Benjamin, and then make out with Mom when she got home, and after dinner play the piano and sing. Now he gets home really late and never plays the piano anymore. It's been over a week since the last time he sang or even smiled. He and Mom talked all hushed after brunch yesterday, and he chewed on a toothpick, which Mom hates. I stood in my doorway, trying to hear. He shoved back his chair so it hit the wall and yelled, "I don't know! I just don't know!" and stomped up the stairs. I hid under my bed so he wouldn't catch me spying.

LATER, I heard Mom on the stairs. I can recognize each person in my family by their footsteps, so if I ever go blind I'll know who's coming. Mom said as she passed my room that I should get ready to go to her mother's house for the party, and she went in to dress Benjamin. I personally believe a nine-year-old should be able to dress himself.

I put on jeans and a sweatshirt. All right, I knew that was inappropriate, but I really didn't feel like getting all dressed up for family. Benjamin was having a temper tantrum because Mom wouldn't let him bring his iguana to the party.

It's always the same scene. Sometimes I think *I* should be the psychologist. He acts stupid; Mom yells at him; he yells and curses at her (*really* curses). She tells Dad. Dad comes to Mom's rescue by screaming at Benjamin, who gets even more hysterical and dumps all his books out of the bookcases and throws his toys around the room. Then Mom yells at Dad for being too hard on Benjamin, and Benjamin is all happy because Mom and Dad get in a fight and Mom's on

22

his side and he's the center of attention again. It's so predictable it's embarrassing.

In the middle of this, while Dad was doing his part, Mom came in to check on me. I was sitting on my bed, covering my ears to block out the fight. She came over and said, "Get dressed!"

"I am dressed."

"You're wearing *that*?"

"Looks that way." I knew that was fresh, but after what my brother had been saying to her and calling her, it was nothing.

"Don't be fresh," she said, predictably. "How about that cute white polka-dotted dress we got for the first day of school?" It was the first time she had asked about it, so she had no idea the garbagemen hauled it away from the Rosensweigs' a week and a half ago.

"No way!" No Wonder.

"Why not? It's perfect!"

"It sucks!"

Neither of us could believe I said that. She whacked me, hard, across the face. I didn't cry. She did. She apologized, about a million times. It was the first time I've ever been slapped—my parents don't believe in it. The thing is, I deserved it. She shouldn't have apologized. She went into her room and closed the door. I bet she threw herself on her bed and cried.

We were late to the party—it took us a while to

collect ourselves. The whole family is a mess. Everybody is angry at everybody else and nobody knows why, or at least I don't. This just doesn't seem to be our year.

The party wasn't as awful as I thought it was going to be, because my cousin Audrey was there. She's a senior in high school and she's great. She taught me about French kissing when I was in fifth grade. It still sounds sick to me. She said it's sort of like "Slap me five" but with tongues instead of hands. I don't think my tongue is that coordinated, so I hope I never have to do it or I will definitely make a total fool of myself. As soon as I walked into Gram's house, Audrey pulled me into the bathroom and asked me if I still have an outie.

The fact that I have an outie has been a huge source of embarrassment for me my whole life. It's hard to decide if I want to wear a bikini, so it shows, hanging right out there for everybody to see, or a one-piece, where there's this little mysterious lump sticking up in the middle of my stomach. Either way, it's pretty gross. I wear a T-shirt when I go swimming with friends and tell them I burn easily. Nobody really says anything when they see it, but you know they're thinking how gross it is and maybe the doctor screwed up when I was born or something. But leave it to Audrey—she just came right out and asked me if I still had an outie.

I told her of course I still had it—what was I going to do, cut it off? If I could, of course, I would. I tried to cut it off with a butter knife when I was about four. My father told me I couldn't, because all my innards would drip out and I'd go flying around the room backwards like a balloon when you untie the knot. Audrey said her friend Crystal had had an outie, but she taped a penny to it for a month and it turned into an innie, so she wanted me to tape a penny to *my* belly button.

If it had been anybody else, I never would've even discussed my body oddities, but Audrey's the kind of person who's just very blunt and says what's on her mind without being embarrassed or letting anybody else be. Also, Audrey has a really excellent belly button, so she knows about these things.

Now I'm lying in bed, not sleeping, with a penny taped to my belly button. I'm leaving it there until I have an innie. I wonder (ugh) how long it will take, and if I'll wreck the chemistry by taking it off occasionally to check. Am I supposed to leave it on in the shower? The tape will get all disgusting. I'll call Audrey tomorrow and ask. She takes these things really seriously and she'll be mad if I do it wrong. I wish she were my sister.

6

DAY OF DREAD. Friday. If I still had friends, I'd be getting ready for Sheila's party right now. I'd have gotten a new big sweater so if anybody kissed me he wouldn't feel the penny. I might be putting on a tiny bit of lipstick. Not enough to look slutty, but just a bit. Then again, I know they'll be playing kissing games, so I probably wouldn't want to wear anything that would smudge all over whoever. Of course, it's pointless for me to spend my time worrying about whether or not to wear lipstick to a party I'm not even invited to.

Today Conor asked me if I needed a ride for tonight. I almost cried right then and there. We were at lunch. I've been saving my homework for lunchtime and doing it in the library to avoid the torture of the cafeteria. So I was walking down the hall to the library and there was Conor, just sort of hanging out by the library door eating a peach. He looked really cute like that, but when he asked me if I needed a ride, I bolted—didn't say a word and went straight into the library. He followed me in, which would have been very sweet and romantic if he liked me and said, "Hey, beautiful, what's on your mind? Something bothering you?" But no. It wasn't like that at all. Instead, he practically snarled, "What's with you?"

"Nothing," I lied.

"Well, you sure got stuck-up all of a sudden," he yelled, and stormed out. Ha! Me? The social reject, stuck-up? I wish!

On his way, he spit out the peach pit, and it missed the garbage pail. If I hadn't been feeling so lousy, I would've thought that was really funny. The librarian yelled at him and dragged him back over to pick it up and put it in the bucket. You're not allowed to eat in the library, especially something like peaches, because the pages of the books will get stuck together. Conor was completely Eleanor Roosevelt. He didn't look back over at me. He never, ever gets in trouble. Today might have been the first time of his whole life. I bet he even makes his bed every morning and never throws his clothes on the floor.

But if he's so perfect, how could he not know I'm not friends with those girls anymore? Who am I kidding—I'm not friends with anyone anymore. Isn't that obvious to him? I'm always alone now. Well, I guess that's not so bad. Maybe I'm a loner. There are definitely some advantages. Nobody interrupts me with annoying phone calls now. I never have to compromise or cooperate. I never have to be considerate of someone else's feelings. I can sit on the curb and cry by myself and nobody cares.

I was walking home from school today (alone, of course) when I saw the bird. It was hanging in the air, still as could be, with one wing pointed up and the other toward the ground. As soon as I saw it, I stopped walking. We were sort of locked in the stillness together. But then I was moving closer, without even meaning to, staring at the bird who had frozen in midflight. I thought at first it was some kind of weird omen, or miracle, but then, when I was almost under it, I saw the kite string. It was caught between two trees. Maybe it was mine, or Sheila's. We used to fly kites together a lot on this street.

The bird's top wing was caught on the string, and his dead body was hanging from it. I stood there, imagining the bird flying around carefree this afternoon, going out to meet his bird-friends down the road

28

without a clue that soon everything would change. Maybe he was a daredevil bird, trying out some new stunts—diving and spinning, twirling and climbing, then diving again. . . . Maybe he was an adventurous bird who flew hundreds of miles, speeding as fast as his wings could take him down this street, which seemed new and exotic to him. Or maybe he'd flown over this street a million times before—maybe he was born here, like me, and wasn't thinking today was going to be any different from yesterday or the day before. And then, suddenly, the invisible kite string tripped him up. Wham! Everything changed, just like that.

I'm sure he panicked. I forced myself to imagine a furious fluttering of his free wing and violent, jerking spasms of his little gray body. How could he possibly know what to do? He'd never been trapped before. Do birds think about God? Do birds think? Does God think about them? Did God tell the bird not to worry, or was he too busy with more important things? Maybe the bird comforted himself by remembering songs his mother used to sing him before he could fly. But either way, I guess, he eventually gave in to the inevitable, and just hung there still as the life seeped bloodlessly out of him.

The thing that got me most, though, the most sickening thing of all, was the other birds. They were chirping. All the other birds in the neighborhood were just singing away happily and beautifully as if nothing had happened. Their friend was hanging dead in mid-air, and nobody gave a damn. They just went on singing. I sat down on the curb and cried for the randomness of it all.

7

OH, MY GOD! Conor just called. He has never called me before, and he just called me. Twice. Oh, my God, oh, my God, oh, my God!

When the phone rang, I put my head under the pillow. I figured it couldn't be for me, because everybody I know is on their way to Sheila's and knows I'm not, so why would they be calling me? Unless it was Wheezy. That's who I figured it was when my mom said it was for me. Wheezy grabbed me as her partner in science class today. Yuck. Sheila worked with Conor, and I was stuck with Wheezy. She's psyched because she knows I used to have friends and now I'm just like her. No! I am not like Wheezy!

I was going to ask my mom who it was, but on the

very slim chance that my nosy mother hadn't asked the mystery caller to identify herself, I didn't want her knowing I was being called by the biggest reject in school—with the possible exception of myself, of course. I was trudging downstairs when she practically sang, "It's a boy. . . ."

I grabbed the phone from her and went into the kitchen closet. I always go in there to talk on the phone. Sheila used to say I sounded like I was in the toilet bowl, but it's the only way to get any privacy in my house. When I realized it was Conor, I kept my fingers crossed that he wouldn't think we had a phone in the bathroom and he'd caught me at a bad time.

I was so surprised to hear from him, especially after the library peach-pit incident, that I think, looking back, I was a little rude. I said, "Why are you calling me?" I didn't want to sound snotty, but it might have come out that way by accident.

He stuttered a little and said "um" a lot, and finally he asked me for the math homework. I had to ask him to repeat it; you can't hear that well in the closet, and besides, how weird! First of all, he never forgets to write down the homework. He's Conor O'Malley— it just isn't possible. And math is his best subject. I think he does it during class. Second, it's Friday night. Nobody—not even a brain like Conor—does homework on Friday night. I mean, I might have to do some tonight to keep myself from jumping out the window, but he has plans tonight, and he knows I know it. Also, I saw him writing down the math homework in class today. Not that I sit and stare at him all the time, which I do, but today I was particularly watching him write down the math homework and trying to copy the way he did it. He's a lefty, so it looks like he's writing upside down. Anyway, I knew for sure he had the math homework.

After I said, "The math homework? You're calling me for the math homework?" he hung up. I felt so stupid. Maybe he's right. Maybe I have no friends because I'm a total jerk. Who would want to be friends with a person who makes them feel like an idiot? So I was just sitting there in the closet on the vacuum cleaner with the phone on my lap thinking maybe I could just stay in there forever when the phone rang again. I was so surprised, and the ring was so loud, echoing as it does in the closet, that I jumped. That caused me to slam my head into the shelf, which was right above me, and knock a major portion of the family's canned food products onto the floor. They were slamming into each other and me, and my mom was yelling, "What's going on in there?" and in spite of myself I had to laugh. I was chuckling and trying to grab the cans when I picked up the receiver and realized it was Conor again.

That surprised me so much I dropped the phone. Then, of course, I had to search around for it among all the cans on the floor, which wasn't easy, because the light was off. I prefer it that way when I'm on the phone, but right then a bit of light would definitely have helped. I was laughing, really laughing for the first time since I started junior high.

He asked if he'd caught me at a bad time, and I remembered about the toilet bowl thing, which got me serious right away. He said he wanted to apologize for hanging up on me and for lying. He said he didn't really need the math homework—he had just panicked when I said hello. That made me like him more than ever. I kept telling myself to stay calm while I asked why he really called. I was hoping he'd say the only reason he was even thinking of going to that party was because he thought I'd be there, and since I obviously wasn't going, he wasn't, either. Or at least maybe he would say he hated the SCANTA girls, so he wasn't going to the party and had called to advise me not to go, either, because everybody was boycotting it.

Fat chance. He said that after the library incident he had bumped into Sheila in the hall and asked her what was up with me. Sheila said, "How should I know? We're not really friends anymore."

I knew that. I know I knew that. We haven't even talked to each other in weeks. But just to hear it like that, third person, so absolute and factual, I felt like

I got punched in the stomach by Mike Tyson. I couldn't talk. I could barely breathe. Anyway, Conor was calling to see what had happened with us.

What could I tell him? I didn't know. I still have no idea what happened between me and Sheila. What had I done wrong? Why doesn't she like me anymore? Why doesn't anybody like me anymore? Why, why, why? I tried to say something cool to Conor, but every time I opened my mouth I had Quiver Voice (Queen Victoria). I tried to say, "We just drifted apart. These things happen. No biggie." As I was struggling to get that out, he asked, "What's wrong?" Well, that did it.

All the very uncool things I was thinking poured right out, between gasps for air and sniffles and snuffles and other horrendous crying noises. He probably thinks I'm nuts. He probably regrets ever calling me. He asked if I wanted him to stop by on his way to Sheila's. Knowing that my eyes were red and my lips were hot and puffy and my nose was running, I said no. He said okay, the big jerk. He obviously doesn't like me. If he liked me, he would've come over anyway. Boys are so dumb. They never have a clue what's going on.

He asked what I was doing tomorrow. What did he think? I have no plans for the rest of my life. He said he and Jordy were going down to the crick, and I could come if I wanted. Pity? Oh, what do I care? I guess I'm a pretty pitiful person. So what if they're going to spend tonight kissing other girls, knowing I'm home, sitting by myself in a dark closet surrounded by dented cans?

8

THE NEXT DAY I went down to the crick. Conor and Jordy were there, racing pieces of Styrofoam through the tunnels to Troll Hole, where the crick goes underground. There isn't much water in the crick this time of year, so the Styro-racers get stuck sometimes, and you have to crawl into the little tunnels that go under people's driveways to poke them through. We're not allowed to do it, because supposedly somebody died in one of the tunnels a few years ago, but I don't know if I believe that.

Jordy found me a piece of Styrofoam and said they'd start over. I hadn't done Styro-racing since fifth grade, and I had just washed my hair and blown it dry, which I almost never do, and put on my best jeans, so I wasn't sure. But then I thought, Why not? I used to be champ at Styro-racing.

And it was fun. I worried the whole night before that they'd talk about all the kissing games at Sheila's, and quiz me on how it felt, being unpopular. They didn't even ask. That's the thing with boys—they can just play or hang out or whatever and not need to know your deepest secrets.

Conor and Jordy got a little ahead of me at one point. Their Styro-racers were neck and neck in the last tunnel before Troll Hole, the one under the Rosensweigs' driveway. The boys scrambled into the tunnel, pushing each other, each trying to get to his racer first. Jordy tripped Conor and Conor fell, pulling Jordy down with him. They were rolling around in the muck, fighting and laughing, forgetting completely about the racers and me. For a minute, I just stood there and watched. They looked so happy. I bet they'll be friends forever.

There I was, the lonely loser again, poking at my Styro-racer with a branch, standing dry and clean on the edge of the crick. Conor and Jordy had pushed themselves back through the tunnel toward me, their racers abandoned behind them. I decided, all of a sudden, that I was going to win. I knocked my Styro-racer loose from the muck and ran past the boys, poking it, splashing through the muddy shallows and under the Rosensweigs' driveway to the other side. I was laughing and breathing hard and starting to sweat but not caring. I have no idea why I suddenly needed to win, since from the beginning I had only gone down to the crick for lack of anything better to do. I haven't cared about Styro-racing in years, but I wanted to win right then. Nothing else mattered.

Just before Troll Hole, I went facedown into the crick. Jordy had tackled me, and he and Conor were covering my face with mud. I thought for a second about my clothes and my hair and the penny that could be torn away from my belly button if they didn't stop it. I think I started yelling at them, but that was stupid because I just got more mud shoved in my face that way. So I decided not to worry about it. I started laughing like a kid, squishing mud into Conor's Orange Crush hair. I straddled his stomach while Jordy fed him mud pies, and it was like we were all back in elementary school.

Then Jordy crawled away toward the Rosensweigs' tunnel. Conor stared up at me, breathing heavy and soaked through with mud. I felt his ribs moving under my legs. I swallowed. He put a muddy finger through my belt loop and my insides turned liquid.

Jordy blindsided me suddenly with a flying mud pie, which knocked me off Conor and back into the crick. Mud and muck and arms and bodies flew everywhere, and the battle raged. The three of us were laughing so hard we had to stop to catch our breath. We sat on the edge of the crick, all covered with mud. Nobody said anything for a long time.

Finally Jordy smiled that electric smile of his, muttered, "Gotta go," and left. Conor saw my elbow was bleeding and asked if it was okay. I hadn't even noticed. I was just feeling good.

Conor and I sat there on the edge for a few more minutes, and then, since my house was on the way to his, he walked me home. We didn't say anything, just walked along together. It was nice. He left me dripping mud on my driveway with a "See ya" and a touch on my back. It wasn't a slap like he gives Jordy—it was gentle. I got that liquid feeling again. I pretended I was going right in but then sat on the steps for a while, thinking about nothing in particular as the mud started to cake.

IN THE two weeks since then, Conor and I have been hanging out more often. I wonder (ugh) if he is my boyfriend. I mean, he hasn't asked me out, but it's not like when my mom was young and people went on "dates." Today is different. But doesn't he have to ask me to make it official? Then again, if he did ask me, who would I tell?

Last year I would've told Sheila and Mom. Obviously Sheila is out, but I can't tell Mom now, either. After supper, she tried to ask me what happened between me and Sheila, but I said I didn't want to talk about it. She asked me if Conor is my boyfriend; I said, "Leave me alone!" and slammed my door in her face. I don't know what's the matter with me. Besides Conor, Mom's the only one being nice to me, and I just push her away. I'm angry at her even though she didn't do anything.

Between classes yesterday, Conor said that he's sick of SCANTA. I said me too. I bet he was jealous because they were paying so much attention to Jordy, who was wearing a pink polo shirt. SCANTA was going bananas. He did look cute, I have to admit. Tracy teased him about it all day. She kept singing, "Hey, there, Jordy Girl." He smiled at her and made her giggle. Why wasn't I that cool when she started in with the Wonder thing?

At the end of the day, I was waiting for Conor by his locker, since we were going to my house to do math together. He came up the stairs from gym, with Sheila bouncing along beside him. I banged the locker softly with my foot so they would notice me. "Okay? Don't forget," Sheila said, and ran over to SCANTA without looking in my direction. Conor got his books, and we walked to my house.

"What did Sheila want?" I asked, once we had arranged ourselves on my floor and started working. What if he said she was his girlfriend and I've been making a fool of myself this whole time? I chewed on my pencil.

"What are you talking about? Did you get x squared equals one fifty-four for number seven?" he answered.

"Today on your way from gym." I was only up to number three.

"Oh. She was asking if Jordy liked Tracy. How should I know? She told me to find out. I think that's wrong."

"Well, you are his best friend. . . ."

"No, not that. One fifty-four. That doesn't make sense."

"Well, does he?"

"Does who what?" It's amazing how algebra could be more interesting to him than the future of his best friend.

"Jordy! Like her!"

"Oh. Yeah, I guess. I don't know. Here it is! I forgot I borrowed from the nine. Stupid, stupid. It's one *forty*-four. Twelve squared. Is that what you got?"

"Huh? Oh, yeah," I lied. "Twelve squared."

9

I'M IN A CLUB. In fact, I'm the president. In fact, I'm all the members. The name of the club is TEBHMAIHEBB. The Every Body Hates Me and I Hate Every Body Back club. We even have a club song: "Teb, hmai hebb, teb teb teb. Hmai hmai hmai hmai, hebb hebb hebb." Pretty catchy, huh?

I think Conor is going out with Sheila. They were partners in science class again yesterday and they giggled the whole time they were counting aphids. I could just throw up. I couldn't wait to get out of there and go to the library for lunch so I could sit alone and write in my journal. I tried to tell myself nothing was definite. Maybe they just thought there was something hilarious about counting aphids.

Well, Jordy and Tracy are a definite. I walked by

the SCANTA lockers this morning, and there was Jordy with his arm around Tracy. It was only eight o'clock in the morning, and there he was, with his arm right around her shoulder. Tracy, of course, said, "Good morning, Wonder!" I know it wasn't my imagination that she said it even louder and snottier than usual. I ducked my head practically down to my looseleaf and kept walking. Jordy said hello and used my real name, I think, but it's impossible to hear him, anyway. He was saying something, but I couldn't make it out and I just wanted to get away from those stupid SCANTA lockers as fast as my feet could take me.

I slumped into my chair when I got to English. K.T. put down her book and took off her glasses. That's Miss Turner, the new English teacher. She's twenty-three, only ten years older than we are, about. She's really pretty. I call her K.T. for Kathleen Turner, since that's who she reminds me of. I don't know her actual first name.

"Good morning, Jessie!" She calls me Jessie. I hate that—reminds me of Dressy Bessie. Last year I would've put a stop to it the first week of school, but at this point being called anything but Wonder is an improvement, so I let her slide. I hear people mellow with age. Maybe that's happening to me.

I looked up for a second, then flicked my eyes back down to my desk. I didn't want to be mean to her.

She's really nice and plus, being new, she's sort of tense—trying to be tough enough to do a good job and still be cool with us at the same time. But teachers, when they try to be your friend, can be so annoying! They tell you they remember being your age, and this too shall pass, and do you want to talk about it. I just wanted her to leave me alone. I didn't need her feeling sorry for me; I was feeling bad enough for myself. I don't even know why I was upset. It's been a rumor since the day after he wore the pink polo that Jordy was going to ask Tracy out. I heard SCANTA talking about it all week at their lockers. It was only a matter of time. And I liked Conor better, anyway.

"Fridays can really be a bummer, can't they?" That surprised me. It didn't sound like a very teacherish thing to say. And she didn't say anything more. Just put her glasses on again and went back to reading her book. Nobody says "bummer" anymore, but I appreciated the effort. She's not bad, ol' K.T., I thought.

Tracy sits right in front of me, so I couldn't miss her doodles: Tracy & Jordy. Jordy + Tracy. Oh, puke. She tore out a page, and I couldn't wait to see what other nauseating things she might scribble. It was not what I expected:

Conor—
Tell the truth. Do you like Sheila?
    P.S. I saw you catch her twice in RCK.

45

RCK! I can't believe it. They played Run-Catch-Kiss at Sheila's party? I thought it would just be Spin the Bottle. What if her parents saw? And if Conor caught Sheila, it means he kissed her. It also means he chased her around her yard for the *chance* to kiss her. *Twice.*

As I was peeking over Tracy's shoulder, K.T. caught me. "Eyes on your own paper, please, Jessie," she said. So much for her being cool! Tracy turned and fixed me with those eyes of hers. She didn't say anything. She didn't need to. Talk about Eleanor Roosevelt! My face was so hot I thought it might melt off. Even Conor turned around and looked at me.

He and Tracy passed the note back and forth a few times. I was dying to look again, but I just didn't have the guts to try. Maybe I should've. Maybe I'd have been thrown out of class and sent to the principal and Mom would have had to come get me and they'd tell her they've had enough trouble from our family and we'd have to transfer to another school district. Oh, well.

I CHOSE to run laps in gym instead of play tennis, and then I cut science and went to the library. That means a zero on homework that I had—all finished—in my notebook, and a chance of being suspended if I was caught, but there was no way I could deal with the happy couple and their aphids again.

The bell rang to end third, but I didn't move, because seventh grade has lunch fourth, so I just sat there writing in my journal.

Tracy pulled up a chair and sat at my table. I slammed my book shut. Just what I need is Tracy Tucker reading about my private life.

"I know you saw what I wrote to Conor today." She was leaning so close I could smell the Dentyne in her mouth.

"So?" I was trying to play it cool. Meanwhile, my hands were shaking so much I had to sit on them.

"Everybody knows about you and Conor."

"What about us?" I thought for an irrational second she might say he and I were going out.

"About how you've been making a fool of yourself, chasing after him."

Part of my right cheek started to twitch. I tried to suck in on it to make it stop.

"Well, I wanted to give you some advice," she whispered. "You better stop because he likes Sheila, and I don't think it would be very nice of you to stand in the way. And besides, you really have to learn when to give up."

Luckily, she left after that. I watched her swish away in her sweatpants and high tops, with her ponytail swaying from side to side in perfect rhythm out the back hole of her SCANTA hat. I waited till she left and then put my head down on my books. I didn't cry. I just sat there for a while and then went to the nurse. No way was I making it through the rest of the school day.

I told the nurse I had stomach cramps, which was the absolute truth. She told me my eyes did look red and watery, so maybe I'd caught the flu. She took my temperature and said I had none, which I suppose meant I had a normal temperature, or else I'd be very dead. She asked me if I was menstruating. Great— just what I felt like discussing. No, I said. Have you started, she asked. No, I yelled. Just what I needed today was the school nurse mocking me for slow development.

I think I made her nervous, yelling like that. She called my mother and said she thought I was coming down with something, so Mom should come get me as soon as possible. I thanked her, smiled, and went to the lobby to wait.

There I was, standing in the lobby, praying for my mother to hurry up, when Conor came down the hall. After the thing with Tracy, I didn't even want to look at him. The bell had rung, so there were a lot of seventh graders coming through the lobby from the cafeteria, including SCANTA. Conor came over and asked if he could talk to me. I wanted to rip his Orange Crush hair out. How could he humiliate me like that in front of all those girls?

I yelled, "Leave me alone, you little geek! I never want to talk to you again!"

I couldn't believe I said it. He just stood there, staring at me. I ran outside. My mom pulled up right then, and I felt like a bank robber making my getaway. I guess that wasn't the most mature way to handle the situation, but for one time this year *I* wanted to be the one to get the last word in. I am sick of being a victim. I don't need friends. "Friend" has *"end"* right in it. Well, I don't want any friends ever again, because "ends" are just too tough.

10

I HAD A ZIT MASK on my face when Jordy came over after school. I was in my room playing Nintendo and warding off acne when I heard my mother talking to somebody at the door, saying she was sorry I couldn't come out but I was sent home sick. Since I could only hear her end of the conversation, I should have known it was Jordy. Him or a giraffe.

Mom closed the door, and he saw me looking out my window, which is right over the front porch. He looked pretty upset, so I opened my window a crack and put my nose on the windowsill so he would see as little as possible of my face.

"Jessica," he said, relatively loudly for him.

"What?" I whispered. Imagine talking quieter than Jordy!

"I gotta talk to you."

"About what?"

"About Conor. He wants— Ew! What's wrong with your face? It's all . . . gross!"

Oops, forgot to stay hidden.

"It's nothing. Just a mask." Trying to sound worldly and sophisticated. Failing.

"Well, it works. It's pretty scary."

"What does Conor want?"

"What happened this afternoon?"

"What do you mean?" I asked, although I knew exactly what he meant.

"Well, Conor was trying to . . . When he finally got you, and you yelled at him like that, in front of the whole school, well . . ." It was the most words I'd ever heard Jordy string together. He was chewing on his thumbnail, looking cute and bashful and probably embarrassed to have said so much. But still, I wasn't backing down.

"Let's just say I'm sick of being made a fool of. Maybe I was too harsh, but you can tell him for me he's humiliated me long enough and I never want to talk to him again."

"He got a nosebleed."

"He what?"

"Yeah. Couldn't go to soccer."

Some people may think that's not all that masculine, getting a nosebleed, but it made me like Conor all over again. That's so cute—he got a nosebleed. The problem with never doing anything bad enough to get yelled at is that when the day finally comes, your whole system goes into shock. But I resolved to stay firm in my hatred.

"That's not my problem."

"Well, I thought you should know he was only trying to ask you out."

What? I was sure I heard him wrong. He was whispering again, and we had my window between us, and . . . *What?* Couldn't be. Tracy said . . .

"Doesn't he like Sheila?"

"Why would he ask you out if he liked Sheila?"

"He didn't ask me out."

"He didn't have a . . . You were yelling pretty loud."

Boy, I sure know how to choose my battles, huh?

"Jordy, was he really?"

"Yeah."

"Well, tell him . . . um . . ."

"He's sitting down by the crick."

"Thanks, Jordy," I said. I plopped down on my bed and started to peel that stupid mask off my face.

He was going to ask me out? Really ask me out? What about Sheila? What about me knowing when to give up? I didn't know what to think. I shut off Nintendo and tried to figure out my next move. He wanted me to be his girlfriend! He was going to ask me out! *Was* is right! Past tense. He probably hates me now. Oh, am I brilliant. Idiot! I know what I'll do. I'll decide what to do and then do the complete opposite, since everything I decide to do is exactly the opposite of what I should have done.

11

I TOLD CONOR about the bird. I know I swore to myself that I would never, that I would keep it a total secret, but I told Conor.

I decided that I should stay aloof and hating in my room, so I washed my face and went down to the crick. Conor was sitting on the edge by the Rosensweigs' tunnel, not moving. I went over and sat down next to him. We both looked at the crick.

"Everything's different—screwed up—this year," he said.

Tell me about it. "What do you mean?"

"Like, we used to race Styro-boats. . . ."

"Well, we did that once, like two weeks ago— remember? With Jordy?" I was chattering and I knew it. I told myself to shut up. Why do I always contradict people when I want them to like me?

"Yeah, but it was . . . different. You know?" He looked at me, then away. "I'm sorry," he said.

"What do you . . ."

"Not about that. I mean for whatever I did to you today."

"Oh," I said. Then we just sat there for a long time again. I knew I should apologize to him for what happened in school, but the longer the silence stretched out, the later my apology was and the tougher it felt to get it out. I didn't know what to say, so I just kept sitting there. My butt was getting cold, but I didn't want to move.

"What exactly did I do, anyway?" he asked.

I started to giggle, and then he did, too. We both started laughing uncontrollably, flopping onto our backs, pounding the dirt with our fists. When we stopped, we both just kept lying there, looking up at the sky. The leaves were beginning to turn. I was breathing deep, smelling somebody's barbecue and digging in the dirt with my fingernails.

"I know about Sheila," I said, finally.

"What about her?"

"About RCK."

"Oh."

That's it? Just "Oh"? I didn't really want to know what happened, but then again, I did.

"What happened?" I asked.

"I thought you knew."

I didn't say anything.

"Is that why you hate me?" He sat up suddenly. "Because I caught her a couple times in Kiss Tag? Who cares? I'm a faster runner than she is."

"Well, you could have told me," I said.

"Why? Why should I tell you that?" He flopped down again. "I know you hate her. I know how bad she hurt you. Why should I tell you a thing like that?"

I couldn't think of a reason. I just kept picturing him running after her and kissing her.

"Anyway, I don't have to tell you anything. You're not my girlfriend, right?"

Obviously not.

"No," I said.

"Do you want to be?"

"What?"

"Do you?"

"What do you mean?"

We were still lying on our backs, looking straight up at the sky. My heart was pounding. "Would you?" he asked quietly. It just hung there in the darkening air above us. A car drove by and beeped impatiently down the road. I felt the cold seeping in through my clothes from the slightly damp ground, and suddenly I could also feel the heat from Conor beside me, on my arm. His hand was about an inch away from mine. I didn't budge.

"Yes," I said, real quietly. Everything was still. The car had stopped beeping. My heart was pounding so loud I'm sure he could hear it. And then, really slowly, his arm shifted across the dirt and he put his hand over mine. We watched the sky darken from pink to burgundy before I said,

"You don't like Sheila?"

"No!"

"You used to."

He didn't say anything for a while. Why do I always push it one step too far?

"Yeah," he said, "I guess I used to."

I didn't know what to say to that, so I just stayed still. I listened to him breathing and got my own breath into the same rhythm. I wasn't thinking about anything except breathing.

"I thought you were gonna beat me up today," he mumbled.

"Sorry."

"I just didn't know what happened, you know? I thought everything was great, that you were pretty normal, especially for a girl, and then—wham! Everything's different."

That's when I told him about the bird.

I told him the whole story of it, except the part of

me sitting, crying on the curb. I told him about the other birds singing while my bird hung there, perpendicular to the street. He sat up and listened. I stayed lying down, staring at the sky. Somehow it felt like the most personal thing I could tell him.

"I don't know why I told you that," I said.

"I'm glad you did."

I sat up, and we looked at each other. Suddenly I thought, Oh, my God, this is it. We're about to kiss. We were moving our faces closer and closer together. My neck was feeling strained because our shoulders were practically touching, so our heads had to turn like ninety degrees to have a chance. How do they make it look so easy on TV? We stopped moving while there was still about an inch separating our lips. I could feel his breath warm on my face and then I couldn't really look at him anymore without getting cross-eyed. I closed my eyes and felt his lips touch mine.

It wasn't at all like being bumped into. It was soft and a little wet, but not at all gross. When I opened my eyes, we were finished. His face was the normal distance away. We both took a deep breath and then we smiled at each other.

"Are you cold?" he asked.

"Not really. How's your nose?"

"Fine." He turned a little Eleanor Roosevelt, and

I silently cursed myself for wrecking another perfect moment.

"That was nice," he said.

"Yeah." My turn for Eleanor.

"Have you ever, I mean, besides in a game, before?" he asked.

"Uh-uh."

"Me either." For some reason, this made us both feel relieved. I noticed he was digging in the dirt with his fingers, too.

"Come on—I'll walk you home," he said, standing, and we started over to my house holding hands. He said he'd call me tomorrow. I wished for somebody to call and tell, but then again, I thought, it's kind of neat keeping it private. It's all mine. I'm going through stuff that Sheila's not part of now. Even if we get to be friends again someday, she will have missed going through all this with me, and it's her own fault. Maybe I'm growing away from her, finally.

When I got inside, Mom said hi in her tense voice. She was reading the paper at the kitchen table, and the whole house smelled like cookies. She always bakes when she's tense.

"How do you feel, sweet?" She doesn't say "sweetheart," just "sweet." I had completely forgotten that I came home sick. She is awfully cool to have let me go out after that. Most moms never would've allowed that. I gave her a big kiss on the cheek, which I haven't done in a long time.

"What was that for?" Big smile. It takes so little to make her happy. I'm such a stinker to hurt her. I resolved never to do it again.

"Just 'cause I love you, Mom. You're the best."

I ran up to my room before the whole situation could turn too sappy. Now I'm just lying on my bed, thinking about Conor and how great everything is.

12

TONIGHT DAD CRIED. It was the first time I ever saw him do that. He said we needed to have an important family meeting, and all of a sudden I was sure that somehow they'd found out about Conor and me and what we did today down at the crick, and that I was going to get grounded until I'm thirty-five. But it turned out the meeting had nothing to do with me. I could kick myself sometimes for being so self-centered.

My dad said he's been working late so often recently because he's been "going over the books." Big N Pretty was losing money like a balloon with a tiny hole loses air, he said, and he was looking for the hole so he could patch it up before everything got deflated. Well, he found the hole. The hole is his partner, Uncle

Tommy. He's not really my uncle, but he and my dad went to college together. Dad thought they were best friends. I guess I could've taught him a thing or two about what best friends do to you.

Turns out Uncle Tommy has been taking money out of the business without telling my dad. Now the company is in trouble. Maybe they'll go bankrupt. I wonder (ugh) if we'll be on welfare and have to sell our house and live in a homeless shelter. Probably if I'd heard that a month ago I wouldn't have cared— I'd just be happy to move. But now I don't want to move. I'm scared—I don't want to be poor. . . . Maybe I should get a job? What do I know how to do? I can baby-sit for the Tayabjis. I get five dollars an hour—I'll keep one for myself and give the rest to Dad. I'll save it up and give him a hundred-dollar bill for Christmas. He was crying when he told us he didn't know what to do about Uncle Tommy, but that we shouldn't worry. Sure.

My mom was holding his hand. Benjamin asked to be excused. He can't handle too much family time. I just sat there. I felt like I should be old enough to say something constructive, or at least ask an intelligent question. Finally I asked, "Why do you think Uncle Tommy is doing that?"

"That's a very good question, sweetheart." Dad says the whole "sweetheart." I was proud that I came up with a good question. "I don't know. I think he may be in some kind of trouble."

Talk about mystery! But I could tell he didn't want to answer any more questions. Maybe Uncle Tommy is on drugs. Or maybe he's a gambler and he owes some shady character tons of money and he's gonna get his kneecaps broken. Maybe he's cheating on his wife, Aunt Peg, and he needs money for his love nest. I've read about these things at Sheila's house. Her mom reads the "tabloid press," which is what she calls those trashy papers my mom won't even look at in line at the supermarket. Sheila's mom *subscribes*. So I know a lot about these things for someone my age.

I was considering advancing a few of my theories, but Dad said, "We'll work it out, sweetheart. Don't worry about it," and looked down at his plate. I stood up and kissed him on the forehead like he used to do to me when I was little.

"I love you, Daddy," I said, "and I'm proud of you." I know that's a stupid thing for a kid to say to her father, but I was trying to think of what he said to me that made me feel best, and that's what blurted out.

"I love you too, sweetheart." His eyes started to fill up again, and I decided to beat it before I started to cry, too. Actually, I was already starting. I don't know why—it's just, I don't know. I didn't think fathers cried. He seems so big and strong and smart and confident. I hate Uncle Tommy. I'm never going to forgive him for this.

I went upstairs, sat at my desk, opened my top drawer, and found the index card from the first day of school there. I looked at it and remembered September 9. I thought about the fact that I could've said "Life is tough" to Dad tonight and really hurt him. I didn't want to, though. I ripped up the card and threw it away.

I went into Benjamin's room to see how he was handling it. I thought maybe he'd feel scared. Nine may be too young to handle stuff like this. I'm going to look it up in Dr. Spock.

He was sitting in the middle of the floor playing with his Etch-A-Sketch (Benjamin, not Dr. Spock). I said, "So how's my favorite fourth grader on the planet?" He shrugged. When he's so quiet like that, it's hard to believe he's the same kid who sometimes shouts stuff that would make Eddie Murphy blush.

I sat and watched him for a few minutes. He concentrates so hard. He was working away at the Etch-A-Sketch like he was doing brain surgery. Finally I asked him what in the world he was trying to make. "A circle," he said.

Everybody tries that, I guess. I did. You can't do it. You can try forever, but nobody can draw a circle on an Etch-A-Sketch. It's good for killing time, but you have to realize before you start it's not going to work. Squares, yes, and rectangles, and even triangles, if you're coordinated. But no way can you draw a circle. That's the thing with an Etch-A-Sketch, and you might as well accept it because you'll just end up frustrated otherwise.

I tried to explain this to Benjamin, but he growled at me. That's what he does when he doesn't want to hear what you're saying. I got up and came back to my room. I've been lying on my bed with the door closed for a long time. When she asked, I told Mom I was doing my homework, but actually I'm just lying here thinking again. Five minutes ago, I heard the Etch-A-Sketch slam into Benjamin's wall.

• 13

I'VE GOTTA START paying attention to my schoolwork. I've been in junior high a month now, and there are whole days that go by without a single thought about it. Sometimes I don't even do my homework. I usually still save it for the library, but sometimes Conor stops by, and I'd rather talk to him than think about Cortés or quadratics, so I skip it altogether.

Today we had a substitute teacher in math. It's the first time we've had a sub this year. We love having subs. We don't learn *anything*. Usually they are way dumber than we are, so we feel sort of obligated to do things to them. Lots of times subs end up crying. One time in fifth grade, Tracy and I pretended we were twins, and the sub believed us, because we really do look a lot alike.

When I saw we had a sub today, though, I wasn't as happy as I used to be. First of all, we're not in Rand anymore. If we get in trouble now, it goes on our permanent record and could keep us from getting into college, and besides, obviously Tracy and I weren't about to gang up on him together. Also, he looked young and scared and I felt bad for him.

Mr. Hickey was his name. That made everybody giggle and look at his neck. He was Eleanor Roosevelt like you wouldn't believe. Teachers are so stupid sometimes. There are certain things they should teach these people in Teacher School. Since I wasn't learning any math, I made a list.

THINGS NOT TO SAY TO SEVENTH GRADERS

1. The word "pianist." "Piano player" says the same thing without sending the class into hysterics.

2. The conjugation of the verb "to come." My Spanish teacher did that last week. "I come, you come, he comes, she comes, it comes, we come . . ." I thought we were all going to pee ourselves.

3. "Penal system." Just try convincing us it has something to do with courts and jails.

4. The word "hickey." If it's your name, make up a new one for the day. Nobody'd know the

difference, and at least you'd start off with half a chance.

So ANYWAY, poor Mr. Hickey was spending as much time as possible with his back to the class, totally unaware that there were chalk stains across his butt, writing algebraic equations on the board. This was a prime opportunity, and I wasn't surprised when I heard some girl from Jefferson Elementary say "chop."

I also wasn't surprised that Mr. Hickey kept spinning around trying to catch the wise guys saying "chop" (sort of as if we were playing a game of Red Light—Green Light and Mr. Hickey was it). I *was* surprised, though, when I heard "chop" come out of my own mouth. Tracy spun around and looked at me. I got Eleanor Roosevelt and looked down at my desk. I hadn't said anything in class for so long I think she forgot she was sitting right in front of girl Wonder, class reject.

I heard her say "chop" and then turn around. I couldn't help but look up, even though I knew I'd turn from Eleanor Roosevelt to Princess Grace (Puke Green), since I was sure she would be scowling at me. She wasn't. When I looked up, she was actually smiling, and not a you-poor-reject-I-pity-you kind of smile, but more like a isn't-this-fun-we're-in-this-together kind of way. I figured I must be misinterpreting, but it gave me the courage to say "chop" again, and when Miles finally yelled, *"Timber!"* I joined in when everybody dropped loose-leafs and textbooks flat *(splat!)* on the floor.

What a crash! Mr. Hickey broke the chalk he was using on the blackboard, which made that awful squeak. He stood there shifting from foot to foot and then told us to do the problems after chapter four and hand them in at the end of the period. Tracy asked if we could work in groups, and he mumbled something like, "I really couldn't care less." My grade is famous for sending young, scared subs into early retirement.

Conor moved his desk next to mine, and we started to work together. Tracy leaned over and asked if she could work with us. Conor and I looked at each other. I was going to be shocked, but then again, who wouldn't want to work in a math group with Conor? I said, "Sure." Besides, none of the rest of SCANTA was in the class. Most of the other kids in math are from Jefferson, the other elementary school besides Rand. Kids from Rand don't hang out that much with kids from Jefferson, so Tracy had nobody to work with.

When the bell rang, Tracy actually smiled at me again. "Bye, Wonder. We'll work together tomorrow, too—if Mr. Love Bite dares to come back!" Although she still called me Wonder (ugh), it was the most she'd said to me all year, and it was almost friendly. Maybe it's because I'm going out with Conor, I decided on the way home.

It's not like anybody would ever be able to notice. It's not like we stand at my locker with our arms around each other. It's not like he has my name written across his notebook in Magic Marker. Jordy has JR & TT on one side and TRACY on the other side of his. Conor thinks that's the stupidest thing Jordy ever did, but I think it's sort of romantic. Conor keeps calling him a sissy. He'll never put my name on his notebook.

Going out doesn't seem that different from being friends. I mean, he calls me sometimes after school or at night, and twice we went to the mall and wandered around, but I used to do all that stuff with Sheila. I wonder (ugh) if Jordy and Tracy kiss all the time. Have they gone to second or even further? Except for that one kiss, Conor and I haven't done anything.

I wish I knew what was normal for kids my age. Like what, for instance, do kids my age do for Halloween? It's coming up next weekend. I am definitely too old to go trick-or-treating. I guess the cool kids my age will go to a party at Tracy's, but since I obviously won't be invited to that, I suppose I could put on my same costume from last year (I'm sure it would still fit—I'm going to be 4 foot 9½ till I'm forty) and sit home eating all the candy we're supposed to give out until I throw up. . . . Maybe I'm bulimic. Cathy's oldest sister got that two years ago, and they had to take her to the hospital for a few months. Now Cathy's mother lives in California, and her father is always watching over Cathy when she eats to make sure she doesn't puke herself or take laxatives like her sister. Pretty gross, if you ask me. I don't think I could make myself puke. Then again, I'm not a teenager yet, so who knows.

I WAS only home five minutes before Conor called, wanting to do the English over the phone. Doesn't he ever just have a snack and unwind? We're learning essays, and tonight we have to write one on *Lord of the Flies*, which turned out to be really good and not about bugs at all like I dreaded. So we were talking about how the conch shell represented power and whoever held it had total authority, and I was thinking how that's just like the remote control for the TV in my house, when he asked me what I was doing for Halloween.

"I haven't really thought about it," I lied.

"You wanna go to Tracy's party?"

That made me sort of mad. I mean, I know she smiled and was nice to me today, but it doesn't mean she likes me. She's probably just setting me up to humiliate me in front of her friends again, so they can all have another good laugh. If Conor wants to go without me, that's just fine. I don't really care. It's a free country. He can do whatever he wants. But if he feels guilty about going after they ridicule and humiliate his girlfriend, he shouldn't try to pawn it off on me when he knows I'll say no because I'm not invited.

"No, thanks," I said.

"Why not?" Boys are so incredibly dumb.

"Well, for one thing, I'm not invited. And for another, I wouldn't want to go even if I were invited."

"I could ask her if it's all right if you come. . . ."

"Don't you dare! Oh, my God! If you do that, Conor O'Malley, I will never, ever speak to you again!"

"Fine. Okay. I won't. I thought you guys were getting to be friends again."

"We're not. She hates me, and I hate her. She was just using me." I wasn't as sure as I sounded about that, but my logic was so convincing it all started to seem obvious.

"Sorry."

God, how humiliating would that be? To have a boy ask your ex-friend if you could come to her party? If she said yes, it would only be out of charity to him, not because she wanted me there, and if she said no—oh! That is the worst! That's way worse than not being invited at all! I'd be so embarrassed. Well, at least I put a definite stop to that. There is *no way* Conor is asking now.

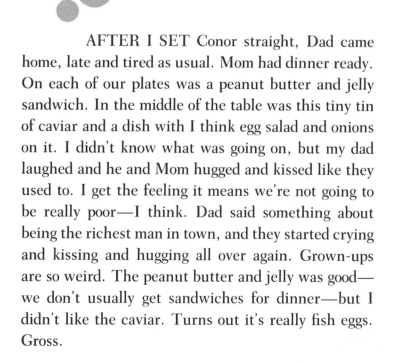

14

AFTER I SET Conor straight, Dad came home, late and tired as usual. Mom had dinner ready. On each of our plates was a peanut butter and jelly sandwich. In the middle of the table was this tiny tin of caviar and a dish with I think egg salad and onions on it. I didn't know what was going on, but my dad laughed and he and Mom hugged and kissed like they used to. I get the feeling it means we're not going to be really poor—I think. Dad said something about being the richest man in town, and they started crying and kissing and hugging all over again. Grown-ups are so weird. The peanut butter and jelly was good— we don't usually get sandwiches for dinner—but I didn't like the caviar. Turns out it's really fish eggs. Gross.

After dinner, I walked up to the Tayabjis' to baby-sit. They go out to dinner on Thursday nights, so I baby-sit for their five-year-old, Kate. Twelve more dollars for my Dad Fund.

Kate was playing with her new Barbie Deluxe Beach Condo. I sat on the couch and watched. Usually I play with her the whole time—I never talk on the phone or anything. I take my responsibilities seriously.

I should be over it by now, I told myself. It's been almost two months. I don't know why I keep torturing myself thinking about Sheila. But little things keep reminding me of her. I'll be going along just fine, and then something comes up that makes me think of her again, and I start asking why, why, why.

This time it was Sheila's tenth birthday. She's three months older than I am, so she got into double digits before me. I went over for brunch and to see what her parents got her—a Barbie Deluxe Beach Condo, just like the one Kate was playing with tonight. We had both been begging for it; it was the big thing that year. The only problem was, Sheila's parents didn't buy her any Barbies.

She never said anything because she didn't want to make them feel bad. I mean, here they bought her this really expensive thing, and they didn't get her anybody to populate it. But they're older than most parents. I don't think they were trying to be cheap or cruel—they probably just didn't know that Barbies aren't included. We called it the Barbie Ghost Town.

It's just like Sheila never to tell them. Even though I hate her now, I have to admit that deep down she's a pretty good person. I miss her. I wonder (ugh) if she ever misses me.

After a while, Kate came over and sat on the couch next to me. She said, "Let's play Ernie and Bert. I'll be Ernie and you be Bert."

I smiled at her. "Okay."

"You have to say 'Bert said . . .' " said Kate.

"Okay, Bert said."

"Bert, said Ernie, why do you look so sad tonight?"

"Well, said Bert, I don't know," I answered in my best Bert voice.

"Did your mommy yell at you?"

"No. I'm just . . . lonely. Nobody likes me anymore. At least no girls do. I think. I don't even know if they do or don't. I don't like them, either, really, but . . ." Don't cry, said Wonder to herself, not in front of a little kid.

"I like you, Bert. I like you a lot. And anybody who doesn't is a doody-dum-dum. Heh, heh, heh."

"Thank you, Ernie, said Bert." I gave her a hug and wished I could be five again, when everything wasn't so complicated.

15

"HEY, WONDER! Come 'ere!" Tracy yelled. I put my head down practically to my loose-leaf, as usual, and kept walking. Balance, I told myself. It doesn't matter if they mock you. You have Conor, and Kate, and your family. These girls are nothing. They can't hurt you unless you give them the power to. Keep walking.

"Seriously. Come 'ere!" I looked up at her. Maybe she was really trying to be friendly? It was early, so only she and Nancy and Amy were at the SCANTA lockers. Sheila's always late on Mondays because Sunday nights they have Double Feature Night at her house. She doesn't go to bed till after midnight sometimes and she can never wake up on time. We have fish and broccoli at my house Sunday nights, to get a healthy start on the week.

"Come on, Wonder—don't be scared. We're not gonna bite ya," Amy said. She had on purple eye shadow and looked like she was in at least tenth grade. She probably wears a bigger bra than my mother. In fifth grade when Amy ran in gym, Sheila and Tracy and I sometimes whispered, "Shake, shake, shake!" and thought we were incredibly funny. I held up my loose-leaf to hide my nothing and walked over. I wasn't scared of them.

"Listen, Wonder," Tracy said slowly, "I'm having a Halloween party Saturday night, and I wanted to know if you can come."

"Screw you," I said, and ran down the hall to English, trying to hold in the tears. How dare he! I specifically told him not to ask her and now I'm a bigger loser spaz outcast than ever before. She had succeeded in humiliating me, with Conor's help, of all people. Next thing you know my *mother* will be calling other kids' mothers complaining that they should invite poor loser me, just like Wheezy's mother used to, before she got tight with the Jefferson girls.

I was succeeding in controlling myself until K.T. came over and asked if I was okay. That is absolutely the worst thing you can do to somebody who's trying not to cry. Boom! I was blubbering right in her face.

She whispered, "Listen, why don't you go wash your face. Hang out in the girls' room till you feel better. If it takes the whole period, fine. Stop by during fourth, and I'll tell you what you missed, and we can talk if you want." Sure. Just what I need is teachers knowing I'm a loser, too.

I went to the ninth graders' wing, where nobody would know me. There were some girls in there smoking. I didn't look up at them. I washed my face and sat down on the windowsill, hoping they wouldn't beat me up for being a seventh grader. The smokers left about a minute after the bell rang without doing anything to me. They'll probably take drugs in high school, drop out, and spend the rest of their lives sitting in doorways with unwashed, snarly hair, mumbling to nobody. What a waste. But I had too much on my mind to start worrying about a bunch of future drug addicts. The one friend I thought I had betrayed me. Serves me right. I should have learned by now not to count on anybody.

Well, this is the last time anyone ever hurts me. Never again. From now on I'm going to be a real loner. I'll hardly ever talk to anybody, and when I do my voice will be rough and hoarse from disuse, so I'll sound mature and mysterious. I'll purposely never have any friends, and I'll live in seclusion, and instead of becoming president of Crayola by slowly acquiring their stock, like I planned, I'll be a world-famous painter. Or sculptor. No—a composer. And I'll compose symphonies of such depth and tragedy people will say, "God, what a talent—I must meet her." But I'll grant no interviews, and people will all think I'm a total genius. And then everyone who hurt me and tormented me and humiliated me will try to bring their children to see me because they will have bragged about being friends with me, and I'll just dis them. They'll be dissed and dismissed. They'll go home humiliated in front of everybody. And I'll think of saying, "You should've been nicer to me in seventh grade!" but then I'll change my mind and not give them the satisfaction.

All that thinking made me feel much better, so by the time the bell rang to go to second period, I practically felt like a world-famous whatever, and nothing could bother me. Then I saw Conor. I saw him see me and smile that cutest smile of his and start to come toward me. I turned around and walked the long way to gym.

WE WERE playing dodgeball, and I was psyched. I wanted to throw that stupid ball right through everybody. I did better than ever in gym, until I beaned Nancy in the head and got sent to sit on the sidelines for the rest of class. I said it was an accident, but I'm not sure it was. Anyway, it was worth it because Nancy got a bloody nose, and I hope it's broken and her perfect little face is horribly disfigured for the rest of her life.

Phew! Where did that all come from? I don't really mean it. Maybe just slightly disfigured. Only kidding. But thinking really awful thoughts cheers me up and makes me laugh to myself. I don't mean them. What if I do? I heard your hormones go nuts in puberty and some people's personalities are radically altered. What if I turn into a psychopathic killer instead of a world-famous composer?

Conor was waiting for me outside gym and he walked next to me the whole way to science. The problem with ignoring him is we have almost the same schedule, so it's tough to avoid him if he wants to walk with me. He kept saying, "What's wrong?" and I just kept ignoring him. Finally he said, "Girls are so damn weird!" and stopped walking. I kept going, thinking he was going to catch up and keep bugging me to find out what he did. What if I become this incredibly fantastic whatever and nobody cares? What fun is that?

I turned around to see what happened to him. He was staring at me, so I had to make it look like I meant to have him catch me. I went right over to him and said, "If you must know, I'm a little annoyed that I asked you *specifically* not to do something, and you had to go ahead and do it anyway. That's what's wrong."

I spun around and walked away, triumphant in my coolness.

"What are you talking about?"

Miss Teller came out of her room and yelled at him for yelling in the hall (like she should talk about yelling in the hall!). If he hadn't been her pet, he definitely would've been booted right to the principal's. He said, "Hey!" and grabbed my arm, which made me drop my books. I would've thought he was a real brute, in addition to being a betraying jerk, but he apologized right away and bent down and picked up all my stuff. He looked so cute and Orange Crushish I almost gave in and started to cry, but I held it.

"I asked you not to say anything to Tracy about me going to the party," I said.

"So I didn't! What, now you want me to?"

"No! You already did!"

"Did not!"

"Did so!" This was getting to be like arguing with Benjamin.

"I swear, Jess, I didn't." I like when he says "Jess." It sounds really sexy.

"Oh, yeah? Well, then, how come she invited me this morning?"

"You got me! Maybe she wants you to come! Did you think of that? Although I can't imagine why!"

He turned bright red, handed me my books, and

walked into class without me. He didn't look at me
the whole period—and we were supposed to be lab
partners. When Miss Teller called on him, he wasn't
even on the right page. First time that ever happened.

I saw Tracy alone at her locker on my way to lunch.
I got up my guts and went over to her.

"Tracy?"

"Screw *you*, Miss High-and-mighty-too-good-to-
come-to-a-party!" she said, and looked away into her
locker. I thought I noticed a little Queen Victoria
and wondered (ugh) what would ever make the in-
destructible Tracy Tucker cry.

"What's wrong?" I asked.

"None of your business, Wonder Bread."

"Fine," I said, remembering I was a psychopathic
killer. "I just need to know why you invited me to
your party."

"Momentary stupidity."

"Did Conor ask you to?"

"You think your little geek boyfriend can tell me
who to invite to my own house?"

He didn't?

"So why did you invite me?"

"I shouldn't have."

"I'm sorry I said what I did."

"Yeah? Well, it's a little late for that. You already
made a fool out of me in front of everybody."

"I didn't mean to," I said. She was crying, putting her head all the way into her locker, pretending she was looking for something buried in there so I wouldn't see. I couldn't believe it. I made Tracy Tucker cry. I tried to feel good about it, but I really didn't. I guess my career as a psycho is down the tubes.

"You wanna go to the girls' room?" I asked, and she took her head out and nodded. She had blue eyeliner dripping down her cheeks. With her hands balled up into little fists, she rubbed at her eyes like Benjamin does when he cries. She looked like a fourth grader right then. Neither of us said a word on the way to the ninth-grade girls' room.

We didn't say anything until after she had washed her face and reapplied her eyeliner. I watched so I'd be able to put mine on the same, if I'm ever allowed to get some. Then she turned around and asked me if I wanted her to put some eyeliner on me. I heard myself say, "Okay." She told me my eyes would look much better with a touch of liner, and actually, when I looked at my face in the tampon dispenser (it's silver, and since there are no mirrors anymore, that's what the ninth graders use) I had to admit I did look better. We almost smiled at each other. I said thanks and we walked back toward her locker.

I ate alone as usual—in the library—thinking

about how to apologize to Conor again. Sometimes I wonder (ugh) how he can stand me at all. And also, how come, if I like him *so much*, I get mad at him so easily? Maybe I'm in love. Is this what love is all about? Yuck. If so, I can hardly wait for high school, when things supposedly get serious.

I wrote Conor a note explaining what happened and put it on his desk before he got to math. I watched him read it and saw him smile (thank goodness) when he got to the part that said, "I know I am a total wackado but will you please forgive and forget? Your girlfriend, Jess." He wrote back, "Yes you are a total wackado but yes I will forgive and forget. Your boyfriend, Conor." That made me feel much better.

Then, as I was sitting there staring at the back of Tracy's head with my freshly made-up eyes, I started letting myself think about what had really happened this morning. She really invited me! She really wanted me to go! I passed her a note saying, "Is the invitation still open?" and made two boxes—a yes box and a no box—and wrote below them, "(Check one)." She passed it back with an X in the yes box. I thought I was going to burst. I almost forgot to read what she wrote in tiny letters next to the no box. It said, "Don't tell anybody about—you know."

I ripped out a new sheet of paper. It made a really

loud noise, but that didn't matter, because we had another sub. I wrote, "Of course not." She ripped that part off, crumpled it, and sent back a note saying, "Say 'CHOP!' I dare you." But by the time I read it, Miles had already started.

• 16

ACTUALLY, THE IDEA came from Dad, though he'll never know it. I asked him last night, during dinner, if he minds when my cousins call him Uncle Tractor. When he was young, he moved so slowly he drove everybody nuts. Santa Claus brought him a toy racing car one year, and his older brother, Uncle Michael, said, "A race car? That kid's so slow he should've gotten a tractor." From that day on, Uncle Michael has always called him Tractor. When I asked last night if it bothered him, being called that, he said he liked it, but Grandma Hazel, who is up visiting from Florida, rolled her eyes. She told me while we were clearing the table that it was only when my dad started calling *himself* Tractor that he stopped feeling bad and started to like it.

That's where I got the idea. I went to Tracy's party as Wonder Bread. It was a pretty easy costume to make—Mom and I got a huge white garbage liner and taped circles cut from colored construction paper to it. Mom thought it was very creative and original. Grandma Hazel took Polaroids.

I got to Tracy's about eight-forty. I figured it would be better to be a little late than be the first one there besides SCANTA, who were probably over early decorating. Mrs. Tucker greeted me at the door. I think she has no idea who I am. She was dressed up as a slinky black cat, smoking a brown cigarette in a long black holder. Her voice is deep and gruff and a little frightening. She called me "dear" and told me the others were down in the basement so I should just go ahead. On my way down, I saw her boyfriend, dressed as Dracula, mixing drinks for them in the library. Tracy's whole house gives me the creeps.

When I got downstairs, Conor and Jordy were across the room talking to Miles and Doug James, a gorgeous eighth grader from Jefferson who's on Conor's soccer team. Conor looked over and winked at me. I smiled and tried to figure out what to do with my hands, cursing myself for not putting pockets on my costume. I started to walk toward Conor and Jordy, even though there were no girls around them.

SCANTA was over by the CD player. When they

saw my costume, they all started elbowing each other. Sheila smiled at me, and out of habit, I smiled back. Amy started to laugh in this really tough cackle and said, "Hi, Wonder! Well, you guys, at least she knows her place!" I felt a sweat ball roll down my stomach and stick to the tape on my belly button. I was dying to itch it; I crossed my arms. Amy poked Sheila in the ribs, and Sheila looked down at her hobo shoes and tried to laugh along.

"Shut up." Everybody turned around to see who would dare tell Amy to shut up. Tracy. She walked right up to me. "Great costume, Wonder. You crack me up. Want some cookies?" And she led me over to the refreshment table on the other side of the room. "Don't pay attention. Amy always acts this way when she has her period," she whispered, and bounced away.

That made me feel a lot better, having the host bring me in like that. I knew that for the rest of the night every time I looked at Amy I would know she was having her period. I started to figure out how many minutes were left till eleven, when my dad would pick me up.

Conor came over to say hello. He was wearing his soccer uniform, and his body looked excellent. I said, "You look good." He said I did, too, and grabbed a handful of M&M's from the table, because the boys had started to throw some at us from across the room. Conor whipped some back and caught Doug on the ear.

Tracy yelled that they'd better stop or they were gonna be in trouble. They all started going, "Whoa, I'm scared—aren't you?" and stuff like that, but they did stop throwing things. Conor went back over to Jordy and shoved him into Doug.

As I was scooping the M&M's back into the bowl, Tracy said, "Boys our age are so *callow*, aren't they?" I jumped. I hadn't realized she was right next to me again. Then I giggled with her. We learned "callow" this week in English—it means immature. I had no idea why Tracy was being so nice to me all of a sudden, but I wasn't about to ask and I kept promising myself to try not to mess it up. She hates me, really, I thought, and I hate her, too, but right now it wouldn't hurt to be big about it and act nice. I congratulated myself on my lack of callowness.

"Eat the orange ones," she whispered. The orange? Everybody knows about green M&M's, but orange?

"Why the orange?" I asked. "I thought the *green* ones make you horny."

"They do! But who cares about being horny?" I never really thought about that. "The orange ones make your boobs grow."

"They do?" Her boobs were about as nonexistent as mine. "Says who?"

"Amy," she whispered, as if it were a state secret. I looked over at Amy's boobs, and at all the boys who were looking at Amy's boobs, and then back at Tracy. Both of us gobbled up all the orange M&M's as fast as we could. With her mouth full, she said, "Hey, I mean it—it took a lot of guts to wear that costume. Very cool. Sheila and Andi think so, too. C'mon, let's start the games."

She went over to SCANTA, turned down the music, and announced that we were going to play Seven in Heaven. The one with the best costume, she said, got to begin it. We all looked around. Almost all the boys, who thought they were too cool for costumes, came either as bums or sports people. Miles came as a ghost with a sheet over his head, only the sheet was green and blue striped. He's so weird. There were a couple of clowns among the girls, and the Parker twins (from Jefferson) and Cathy were the three blind mice, which was cute except they all looked the same so you couldn't choose one as being best. Sheila and Andi were dressed as hoboes, which was cute but not too creative. Amy and Nancy were dressed as rabbits— Nancy like a bunny rabbit in her feety pajamas with cotton glued on for a tail, Amy like a Playboy bunny, with stockings and black high heels. Tracy was a pumpkin, which I thought was best—it was a round laundry basket covered with orange crepe paper and black construction paper cutouts.

We had a vote. I knew most of the boys were going to vote for Amy's. They whistled and yelped when they voted, and she pretended to be embarrassed, but I knew she loved it or she wouldn't have dressed like that. I nominated Tracy's, and a few people voted for it. I hope nobody thought I was just kissing up—I really thought hers was best. Then Conor nominated me. Lots of people voted for me. I was pleased but also mortified. I didn't want to start Seven in Heaven! I never even played the thing before. "Wonder Bread wins!" yelled Miles. Terrific. I wore the damn thing to prove to SCANTA and myself I didn't care about their stupid mocking, and now I had the whole seventh grade calling me Wonder. *Ugh!*

Everybody was staring at me. "Go ahead, Wonder! Pick somebody!" Even Cathy, who usually speaks about as often as Jordy, was egging me on. Who else would I pick? Conor was plenty Eleanor even before I said his name. We got up and went into the closet, while Miles set his stopwatch for seven minutes and closed the door behind us. I leaned against the door. Conor sat on a pile of old turtlenecks and long underwear. Neither of us said anything. Then I thought, What will everybody think if they're all listening and there's no talking in here? So I tried desperately to come up with something to say. We both started at the same time. I made him go first.

"I just said, you wanna sit down?" he said, looking at his cleats. "What did you say?"

"Oh. Um, sorry about being nasty at school, you know, last week." I had already apologized for it, but I hadn't been able to come up with anything else. I sat down on the clothes pile and I guess shifted something because I started an avalanche. Before I knew it, I was on the floor under a bunch of old clothes. Conor laughed and put out his hand to help me up. When he pulled me up, I was right opposite him. It was pretty dark, but still I could see he was looking right in my eyes and I couldn't for the life of me pull my eyes away. He put his hand on my back, and suddenly we were kissing.

This one lasted much longer than the one at the crick. Our whole bodies were pressed up against each other, and it felt really good. I prayed he wouldn't feel the penny. When we stopped, I could feel him breathing hot air on my face. His breath smelled like Crest. I shut my mouth because I remembered that mine smelled like orange M&M's.

"Wow," he said, all breathy.

"Yeah," I said, and sniffled. It was hard breathing through my nose. I'm generally a mouth breather.

"Can we do it again?"

"Okay," I said, and, my heart pounding, I closed my eyes and braced myself. This time he put both hands on my back and held me even tighter. It was really nice but also sort of scary. I had to push away to get some air, which ripped the tape loose. I felt the penny dangling by one edge of tape. My whole body was shaking. My left knee started to spaz out, and I thought I might knock him with it, so I sat down and tried to retape my penny without Conor seeing, which wasn't easy through the garbage liner. He stayed standing.

"Sorry," he said.

"About what?" What was he talking about? I was the one who should apologize. I didn't know why my body was freaking out like that, and I was desperately trying to get the tape to stick.

"Forget it," he said, and didn't look at me anymore. We just stayed there until Miles opened the door and said, "Stop it in there, you lovebirds!" and let us out. As I stood up, the whole penny apparatus fell off, wiggled through the bottom opening of the garbage liner, and clanked to the floor. I scooped it up fast, before anybody saw, I think. I was more Eleanor Roosevelt than ever, clutching it in my sweaty hand.

It was Conor's turn to pick, and of course he couldn't choose me (not that he would've after I acted like such a baby), so he chose Sheila. I ran to the bathroom and tried to get the penny back on, but the tape was all destickified. I looked down at my outie. No progress so far, and it had already been six weeks. Audrey had called after a month to see how it was going, since it only took her friend that long. She was disappointed and said maybe I was taking it off too often to check. I found two Band-Aids in Tracy's cabinet and restuck it.

When I got back to the party, Conor and Sheila were coming out of the closet. Conor walked straight over to Doug, and Sheila looked a little Eleanor Roosevelt. I tried not to think about what might have happened in there.

While Sheila went back in, this time with Whit Levy, a sort-of cute eighth grader, the rest of us played Spin the Bottle. Jordy got me (he kissed nice and gently—in fact, he barely touched my lips) and I got Miles, who still kissed like it was Bumper Faces. Seven in Heaven went on for a while, and Spin the Bottle, which gets pretty boring, disintegrated. We all just sat around and listened to Tracy's brother's CD player.

My father came to the door at ten-fifty. I had told him to wait outside and I'd come out at eleven, but no. I ran up before he could come down to get me and make it even worse. Mrs. Tucker, the alley cat, was practically purring when she pecked him on the cheek and said, "Happy Halloween." She blew smoke in his face, which I happen to know he hates, but instead of waving it away he just stood there in his Groucho Marx glasses until I tugged him out the door. Mrs. Tucker's boyfriend was in the library mixing drinks. Either he's awfully slow, or he and Mrs. Tucker were getting loaded.

17

BOYS ARE SO CALLOW. Apparently after I left, they got even more rowdy and had an all-out food fight, which Tracy's mother had a cow about—she made everybody wait outside for their parents. Tracy called me this morning to ask if I could come over to help clean up. If the party had been at my house, Mom never would've let me invite somebody else over to clean up afterward. And besides—why me? A week ago she hated my guts! Now, suddenly, I'm such a close friend she feels comfortable asking me to help clean her basement?

I went over there around noon. Andi and Nancy were already there. They were all wearing long sweaters with leggings and clogs. I'm not allowed to get clogs, because my feet are narrow so the clogs would fall off and Mom's convinced I'd crack my ankle. My feet are the only long things on me. They look like they belong to somebody Andi's height. Gram says that means I'm going to grow soon. I wish the rest of me would hurry and catch up. I wish I had short fat feet like Nancy's. Hers are so cute. Sheila used to ask me if I could peel bananas with mine.

There wasn't much cleaning up going on, as far as I could tell. Nancy was polishing her cute toenails, and Andi was French braiding Tracy's hair. That's another lousy thing about me. I have this stubbornly straight hair that is completely useless unless you're coordinated enough to put it into braids or something. I'm a total spaz when it comes to my hair. I usually don't even blow it dry. I just comb it when I get out of the shower and that's it.

Anyway, I didn't know what to do, since they all just sort of looked up and said, "Hi, Wonder," and went back to what they were doing. I started to pick up Fritos from the floor. Andi finished doing Tracy's hair and asked me how it looked. I sat down where I'd been crawling in my new red sweatpants and looked.

"You look great," I said. She really did look pretty like that, so I wasn't just saying it.

"You don't have to do that," Tracy said, talking about cleaning up, not about complimenting her.

"I don't mind," I answered, but stood up and

brushed off my sweats. What to do, where to go, how to stand? Why am I so awkward? My hands are in the way, *always*. They don't know where to go. What do other people do with their hands? I felt like Magilla Gorilla.

"Want me to do yours?" I was wishing from the second I walked in that Andi would ask me that, but I acted cool and pretended to think it over for a while.

"Okay." I shrugged, as if I really didn't care one way or the other. Tracy got up, and I took her place on the floor in front of Andi, who started brushing my hair. I was psyched that I'd decided to wash my hair and use conditioner this morning, even though it wasn't dirty since I'd done it only like twelve hours earlier for the party.

"Where's Cathy?" Nancy asked as she moved on to her second foot.

"All-State Band practice," said Tracy, who was trying to look at her French braid in the mirror of her blush compact.

"With the Parker twins," added Andi. They all nodded, knowingly.

"She sure likes clarinet!" I said.

As soon as that popped out, I wanted to suck it back in. It sounded ridiculous, and it broke the rhythm of their conversation. They all stared at me for a minute, as I turned Eleanor. I decided I'd better stick to "uh-huh" when I agreed and "mmm" when it seemed like I should say something, but I wasn't sure what. My palms were sweating. I sat on them and said to myself, Try to fit in. Shut up and don't blow it.

On the way home, apparently, Amy had told Nancy that she'd gone to second with Jordy during Seven in Heaven. (Mmm.) Nancy called Tracy to tell her first thing this morning. How could Amy let him touch her tits, Andi said. She knew Jordy was going out with Tracy. As Tracy said, Amy was supposed to be her friend. It's really the lowest of lows to choose a boy over your friends. (Uh-huh.) Amy is such a slut, Tracy said. (Mmm.) Satisfying her horniness is more important to her than friendship. I finally came up with something to add. I said, "Maybe she ate too many green M&M's."

That cracked everybody up. At first I wasn't sure if they were laughing at me or with me, but then I decided I should laugh along regardless. Nobody could stop. Nancy made snorting noises, which made us all laugh harder, and by the time we regained control of ourselves, my face and my sides ached. Tracy checked me out and said, "Too bad the orange ones didn't do much for either of us!" That started the laughing fit all over again. I didn't even mind that they were laughing at my flat chest, because I knew Tracy was at least as bad off, and besides, I had caught their rhythm.

"Well, that made me feel better," Tracy said, wiping the tears from her cheeks and taking a deep breath, "but I'm still really mad at Amy. And at Sheila." They all looked at me. Nobody was laughing anymore. Andi started to French braid my hair. They all looked at each other, and wham! There I was, outside it all again.

"What?" I asked really quietly. They all looked down.

"Oh, she'd already left. . . ." Nancy said.

"What happened?" I hate my father for coming early! He's ruining my life! I thought of the twenty-four dollars I'd already saved up to give him and thought maybe I wouldn't.

Andi cleared her throat. "Oh, Sheila was just saying stuff."

"Like what stuff?" I thought about her and Conor in the closet together and how prudish he must think I am. Maybe Sheila . . . "Is it about Conor? In the closet?"

"Yeah," said Nancy. Oh, God.

"She was saying," said Tracy slowly, "how he's such a good kisser, and she should've gone out with him when she had the chance." Terrific. I bet she didn't act all babyish. She always breathes through her nose.

"Terrific," I said.

"Well, if you ask me," said Andi, as she finished

my braid, "they're both a couple of sluts. They know you two are going out with Jordy and Conor. Why don't they try to find their own? I know if one of them tried to make the moves on Doug, I'd never speak to them again."

"You're going out with Doug James?" I didn't mean to sound so shocked, but he is about the cutest boy in eighth grade. Absolutely everybody likes him, but I didn't think he'd even *look* at a seventh grader.

"No, I'm not, but that's not the point. I like him, and, well, they know it." That sounded kind of weak, but I sure wasn't about to argue. I was back to thinking about Sheila making out with Conor, right there in the closet I was sitting next to. I can't believe she actually kissed him. I can't believe he picked her! I tried to decide who to hate more.

"Well, I'll tell you one thing," said Tracy, handing me the mirror so I could check out my braid. "Wonder and I aren't loving those two sluts very much right now. That's for sure." She nodded at me, so I nodded back.

The phone rang. Tracy's mom answered on the first ring. My mom always waits at least for the second, even if she's standing right there, so it won't seem like she was sitting waiting for a call. Tracy explained that her mom always picks up fast, now that she's divorced. I know plenty of divorced people who don't do that, but Nancy said it's pretty common among divorcées. Nancy's stupid but she sounded pretty well-informed on this, so I kept my mouth shut. It was the first half hour I had of junior high semipopularity, and I wasn't about to wreck it debating the phone-answering habits of recently divorced women.

"What if it's Sheila?" Andi asked. "Or Amy?" We all looked at Tracy.

"They wouldn't have the guts to call here."

"What if they do?"

"I'll tell them to buzz off."

"Yeah," said Nancy quietly, looking at her perfectly polished toenails, "but what about SCANTA?" My turn to look down.

"Screw SCANTA," said Tracy. "As far as I'm concerned, SCANTA is dead."

I decided it would be inappropriate to jump up and down.

"Tracy!" yelled her mother. "Phone!"

Tracy stood up and looked at us with Sheila's raised-eyebrows look, spun around, and ran up the stairs. Andi, Nancy, and I sat hardly breathing, waiting to see who it was. I tried to think of something to say.

"You're lucky," Nancy said to me.

"Me?"

"Yeah, I mean, that you have a nickname." I always thought she was dumb, but I swear, I was ready to call Guinness. "I mean," she continued, "I know it started as teasing, but now everybody thinks it's just the cutest nickname ever! I wish I had a nickname. But Nancy already sounds like it's the nickname for something—like Nancella or something." Andi and I cracked up, and then Nancy did, too.

"Nancy, you say some of the dumbest things!" Andi shook her head. Andi is short for Andreya, and even though Andi sounds like a boy's name, Andreya is so—I don't know—so sophisticated it'll fit Andi perfectly when she grows up. She's more Cosmo than anybody in our whole grade—or anybody I know. I should watch her more, I decided, and learn to be less spastic.

When Tracy came back down, we were still repeating "Nancella" and cracking ourselves up. I was thinking about it. Maybe Wonder isn't such a bad thing to be called. I don't know. I'll be twenty-five, going on a job interview, introducing myself as Wonder.

"Wonder?" the president of Crayola will ask.

"Yes," I'll answer politely. "As in bread."

"It was Sheila," Tracy announced. "She wanted to know if she could come help clean up."

"What did you say?" I couldn't believe I was actually feeling some sympathy for the girl who dumped me and then fooled around with my boyfriend.

"I told her no. 'My friends are already here,' I said, and then hung up."

"All right!" we all yelled. I liked being on this side.

Besides, she deserved it. It's great to have friends who will stand up for you. After all, Sheila didn't do anything to Tracy—she did it to me. And these girls were willing to break up the most popular clique in school, partially on my behalf.

We hung around for a while and finally got some of the stuff picked up. Luckily I had convinced my father that I could walk home if I did it while it was still light out. Honestly, they still treat me like a child. And then tell me to act more grown-up—or worse, act my age. What is that supposed to mean? How do people who are almost thirteen act? I wish I knew *how* to act my age.

Then again, maybe I'm learning. I'm suddenly popular again, right? At least I'm now in with the most popular girls in my grade. This is the best thing that could ever happen to me, I decided. Now Sheila probably *will* come crawling back to me, and I'll let her see how awful it feels to be an outcast.

I am on top of the world, I kept repeating to myself the whole way home. I don't need Sheila *or* Conor. Let them be together if that's what they want. Fine. They deserve each other. This is all for the best. I am the happiest girl in the world, and things are just going to get better from now on.

When I got home, I went straight to my room, shut the door, crawled under my covers, and cried.

18

HE STOOD, palms flat on the table, leaning forward.

"Jessica, we need to talk."

"Fine. Talk," I said, raising my eyebrows at Nancy, who started to giggle and choke on her bologna sandwich.

"Privately." He picked up his books and waited for me. What was I supposed to do? I looked at my friends, but they weren't sending any decodable eye signals. I was on my own. Yuck.

"Save my spot," I said, and got up. I left my half-eaten sandwich and my books on the table. Walking out of the lunchroom in silence with Conor, I wondered if I had done the right thing or if they'd be mad.

We'd been ignoring the boys for two weeks. Was that enough?

When we got outside to the playing fields, he sat down. What was I supposed to do? So I sat down next to him.

"Let's talk," he said emphatically. I could tell he'd rehearsed. He looked really cute in his ragg wool sweater and gray corduroys. Don't, I told myself. Don't think about that.

"Fine. Talk." It didn't sound quite as cool this time.

"What's going on?"

"What do you mean?" Damn that Queen Victoria. Do girls' voices change? Maybe that's it.

"I mean, are we still . . . I mean, are you . . . still . . . my girlfriend?" You would think he was asking the kids playing Wiffle ball because that's where he was looking. I watched them, too.

"I don't know," I said, trying to sound blasé.

"Well, do you want to be? Anymore?"

"I don't know." What would Tracy say if it were her and Jordy having this talk? Why did things always get messed up for me?

"Well, it sure doesn't seem it. It seems like all you care about is being a Slick Chick." That's what they called us now. We pretended to hate it, but we didn't.

"What do you want from me?" I asked.

"I don't know."

"Are you saying you want to break up?"

"Yeah, maybe."

Ouch. What could I say to that?

"Are you asking me to choose between you and my friends?"

"I thought I was your friend, too," he said.

"So did I," I said. I felt very old. I leaned back on my hands and watched the Wiffle ball game for a few seconds, although I felt Conor looking at me. Then I got up and started walking back inside.

"What is that supposed to mean?"

I didn't flinch or turn or slow down. I walked right back to the lunchroom, reminding myself I still had some true friends.

My books were at the table with only my half-eaten lunch for company. I grabbed up my stuff and ran right to the lockers. Tracy, Nancy, and Andi were sitting there. I plopped myself down and started talking right away.

"You'll never believe what just happened. . . ."

"I don't think we care," said Nancy.

"What do you mean?" Queen Victoria.

"Look," said Tracy, standing up and closing her locker, "you're going to have to decide who's more important—your friends or a boy."

"What do you mean? I just . . . my friends, of course! You guys, come on!"

"Fine," said Andi, also standing. Nancy and I stood

up, too. I tried to gather my books. "You make your choice. Then stick to it."

We all walked our regular route to class without talking. How could I prove to them I'm like them? I am a loyal friend, and I know it's the lowest of lows to choose a boy over your friends, even if he is your Orange Crush.

• 19

EVERY YEAR it's the same thing. Before Thanksgiving, we always have to write about what we're thankful for. K.T. gave it to us yesterday as an essay test. I just sat there most of the period looking at Conor's work boots. My brain was filled with marshmallows. I am thankful that my brain is full of marshmallows and my belly is not. No. I am thankful that every English teacher asks this same question so I know if I write something mushy about my family and put the commas in the right places I'll get a good grade. No.

Thanksgiving
It is fine to pick a rose
But it's gross to pick your nose

110

Give thanks for poetry, not prose
Because what matters is what shows
by
Jessica Powers

It's one of the worst things I've ever written and it's not even an essay. K.T. probably won't be disappointed, though. I think she's gotten over believing in me as her star student. School just isn't that important to Slick Chicks. The thing is, I know I used to be totally capable of writing an essay that would get an A. I stuck it in the middle of the pile and ran out.

THIS MORNING the Slick Chicks (Tracy, Nancy, Andi, and I) went to the mall to get bras for me and Tracy. Nancy and Andi, while not huge like Amy, already have bras, so they knew how to do it. Tracy and I stood in the dressing room, both Eleanor Roosevelt, taking off our shirts. I had forgotten about the penny—I'm so used to it now, I don't even notice. But Tracy sure did. "What's that?" she asked, pointing.

"A penny," I answered.

"Well, duh. Why do you have a penny taped to your belly button?"

"My cousin told me about it. Everybody in high school does it."

"Why?"

"Oh, Tracy. Don't tell me you don't *know*?" I had no idea what I was talking about. Stalling for time till I could come up with something was all I could think of—that and the fact that if I didn't pull off this moment with some finesse the whole school would know by Monday morning that I have a penny on my outie.

"Of course I *know*. I was just . . . you know. I do it sometimes, too. I just forgot. Today." She smiled. How weird. We nodded at each other, though neither of us had a clue what in the world there was to *know*.

Nancy and Andi came back and handed an assortment of bras under the dressing room door. Luckily Tracy is small like me, or it would have been too humiliating, although I am growing, a little. I'm up to 4 foot 10 and not completely indented anymore. Tracy and I decided we have "mosquito bites."

WE WERE trying to act casual as we strolled across the mall with our white My First Bra bras (size 32 AA) securely in their bags, looking at the Christmas decorations that were already going up. We chose the charms we're getting each other—a little gold 4 to represent the four Slick Chicks. Each of us will ask our parents for a charm holder, too. I already asked Gram if, instead of my usual Christmas gift of a share of Crayola stock, she could get me clogs specially made for narrow feet. It's weird to be thinking about Christmas already, since we haven't even gotten through Thanksgiving yet. It doesn't feel like Christmastime at all.

We were heading over to try on the lipsticks at the makeup counter when we saw Sheila and her mother. Sheila was sitting on a chair in front of Lancôme, definitely wishing the carpet would swallow her up. How embarrassing, seeing a bunch of girls you used to hang out with when you're shopping with only your mother. To make matters worse, Sheila's mother was putting powder on Sheila's forehead to cover the zits under her bangs. When did she start getting zits? She should use my mask. Sheila dropped her bangs and started picking at her cuticles.

"Hi," Sheila muttered when we came up to them.

"Getting some face powder, huh?" Leave it to Nancella to point out the obvious. Sheila's mom tactfully wandered away. She didn't even say hello to me.

"Yeah," Sheila answered meekly.

"Look," said Tracy, in that steely voice of hers, "why don't you give it up? It doesn't matter how your face looks if you're a slut." Sheila just sat there. I saw her tears well up and threaten to spill over, but she and Tracy were locked in a staring contest and neither was about to surrender.

"Hey, Tray," I said, "lighten up, huh?" I couldn't believe that came out of my mouth. What was I doing?

"Butt out, Wonder. This has nothing to do with you."

This had everything to do with me! What was I doing? I couldn't think.

"It does so have to do with me. . . ." That came out way meeker than I intended it to.

"Yeah? Well, you just remember who your friends are." Suddenly Tracy had forgotten Sheila and was staring at me with the dreaded icicle eyes. They sure looked different at our sleep-over last night, when she told me her father forgot to call on her birthday.

I looked at Sheila, who was also looking at me. Remember who your friends are? How was I supposed to remember who my friends are when obviously I've never really known in the first place? Was I willing to throw away these new friendships to defend Sheila, after all she had done to me?

"Of course," I said, poking Tracy with my My First Bra bag. "I'm just saying, let's not make a scene, if you know what I mean." I raised my eyebrows and tried to give her a meaningful look.

"Yeah, you're right." The four of us started to giggle about how embarrassing it would be to get thrown out of the store and have the security guard check our bags. I had turned my back on Sheila to laugh with Tracy, Nancy, and Andi. When I turned around again, Sheila was gone. I guess she went after her mother.

• 20

I JUST HAD my first heart-to-heart with Mom since the beginning of junior high. We used to sit on top of my comforter and have a private talk every night before bed, but I can't let her into all the nooks and crannies of my life now, because I'm not her little baby anymore. The problem is, every time I say that to myself, it makes me cry. I don't know what my problem is. I never used to cry. I used to beat up little boys who picked on Benjamin, and even when I got hurt, I didn't cry. Now I cry every day. The littlest thing can set me off. Or nothing. Sometimes I just cry for no reason at all. I may honestly be losing it.

Tonight, though, I think I was justified in crying. Sheila called me. I was trying on my new bra and checking myself out in the mirror. I was wearing day-of-the-week underwear on the wrong day (Tuesday—today's Saturday), a training bra that had nothing to train, and a penny taped to my belly button. Not the sexiest picture. When the phone rang, I just had a feeling it wasn't Playboy making me a million-dollar offer.

I threw on sweats and went down into the kitchen closet. I was expecting Tracy, so Sheila's voice caught me unprepared.

"I just wanted to thank you, you know, for standing up for me today."

"I didn't stand up for you." I didn't need her thinking she was getting in with us through me.

"I know you didn't mean to, but you're just not like them."

"I am so." How dare she? "And they're my friends. I'd appreciate you not saying anything bad about them."

"Listen, Jessica." It was the first time she'd called me by my name all year. "I just want to warn you. You can't trust them."

"Look who's talking." Why was my voice Queen Victoria?

"I know. I owe you such a huge apology. You're the only true friend I ever had, and I screwed it all up."

"Yup."

"I'm not asking you to forgive me. I'm just saying,

116

I know what you're doing and I think you're making a mistake. I don't blame you for hating me, but Conor is—"

"Don't even talk to me about him."

"Look, Jessica. Nothing happened. I didn't . . . You wanna know what happened? He spent the whole seven minutes telling me I shouldn't be a jerk to you. Okay? I said what I said because, well, you wouldn't understand."

"Tell me."

"Because I thought it was what they wanted to hear. Okay? And also . . ."

"What." No more Queen Victoria. Steel.

"I guess I was jealous."

"Of me?"

"Yeah. You know? You seemed so sure of yourself, and you had a boyfriend who was crazy about you, and I don't know—so I acted stupid. I lied, okay? I wish it never happened, but there's nothing I can do now."

"Nothing happened?"

"Nothing, I swear. It's just, Jessica, don't . . . Well, who am I to give advice, right?"

"Right. Bye," I said, and hung up. I sat there for a while with the phone on my lap. Then I ran upstairs, slammed my door, and flopped, crying, on my bed. I didn't even hear Benjamin come in.

"What'sa matter, Jessica? Why are you crying?"

"Get out! Leave me alone!"

"Do you want to hold my iguana? That sometimes helps me. . . ."

I turned over and looked at him. He was holding out his iguana to me. I hugged my brother really hard. Things are so simple when you're nine.

"I love you, Benjamin," I said.

"I love you, too," he said, disentangling himself from me. He left, petting his iguana. I pulled my covers over my head, so I didn't see Mom come in.

"What's going on?" she asked quietly.

"You're supposed to knock when my door's closed, Mom."

"I know. Your door wasn't closed." Benjamin.

"Oh," I said, uncovering my face.

"You wanna talk about it?" She sat down on my bed, and suddenly I was blurting it all out. Everything. The dress, Sheila, SCANTA, the bird, Conor, the parties, everything. In no particular order. She just sat and listened, occasionally handing me a Kleenex. It felt sort of like throwing up. Once I started, there was no way to hold any of it back until it all came out.

"What should I do? Just tell me what to do and I'll do it." I was too worn-out to assert my independence. I just wanted her to gather me up and rock me like I was her baby again and make it all better.

"Uh-uh. Come 'ere," she said, and pulled me over

to the mirror. I looked at the puffy-eyed, runny-nosed monster staring back at me. "No matter who you're friends with, no matter what you do, *that's* who you'll have to face every day for the rest of your life. Decide what you need to do to make *that* person proud."

She gave me a kiss and walked out of my room.

But what if I'm *not* proud, Mom? I know I have to like myself, but what if I honestly don't? What if my real self is just not likable? What if who I am doesn't fit in, and has an outie, and doesn't know what to do with her hands and wears queer clothes? Then don't I have to change who I am? But if I can just change, then who is me?

21

THE SLICK CHICKS have gone the way of SCANTA and dinosaurs. No big fight or anything—we just didn't do everything together this week, which is all it takes. The Fantastic Four from Jefferson seemed to get a lot of attention in the vacuum we left. I'm trying not to notice.

Yesterday Conor came to the library halfway through lunch and we walked to math together afterward. On the way he gave my sneaker a flat, so I had to kneel down and put it back on. He waited for me, smiling and bumping against the wall. I chased him to class. He almost let me catch him. Maybe all hope is not yet lost, and someday he'll like me again.

As I passed Sheila's locker at the end of the day, I waved to her. She said, "Bye, Jessica. Happy Thanksgiving." I thought about calling her up last night and asking if she wants to go to the mall this weekend, but then I didn't. I think it's going to take some time.

So. It's Thanksgiving. When I woke up, I smelled the onions Mom was frying for stuffing. I opened my eyes, and there was Benjamin, staring at me, waiting. He climbed into my bed with his Etch-A-Sketch and asked me to make him a circle. I couldn't do it, of course, but we laughed a lot. After he left, I counted up my Dad Fund. So far I've saved forty dollars. It probably won't make much of a difference, but I like trying to.

I put the money back in my desk and changed into my red sweatpants, Big N Pretty sweatshirt, and Keds. I wish I hadn't asked Gram for clogs instead of Crayola stock. Knowing me, they really will fall off my feet and I'll go sprawling down the hall with books and lunch and self flying every which way. I don't need extra potential for humiliation this year. I've had enough.

Last night before bed, I asked Mom if she remembered being almost thirteen. "Oh, yes," she said. I asked how it was for her. "It sucked," she said. We smiled.

Before I went down to help make the stuffing, I looked in the mirror. I lifted up the sweatshirt and checked. Still an outie. I took the penny off. I'll have to tell my cousin that it just didn't work for me.

Someday I might be ready to put it back on, when my hormones settle down. Maybe hormones interfere with the copper or something, and if I wear it for a month in high school I'll get an innie. We'll see. For now, I'll just have to stay like I am. Will I ever stick out in the places I should, instead of where I shouldn't? I wonder.